THE GUNS OF
HELL VALLEY

THE GUNS OF HELL VALLEY

JOHN PRESCOTT

CUTTING EDGE

Published by
Cutting Edge Books
PO Box 8212
Calabasas, CA 91372
www.cuttingedgebooks.com

PART I
BY THE GUNS FORGOT

CHAPTER ONE

THERE WAS cloud in the early part of the day, but toward the middle of the afternoon it raveled off, and the sun came through the rifts to pinto-spot the piny mountains and the long, fingering ridges of the foothills that reached out of them. To the east, toward the Pecos valley, the land began to roll and then to level out, and in that direction the grama grass stood up in dark or shining masses, depending on the way the light might take it. All about the rutted crossing of the road in the arroyo where the riders halted, the white dust and limestone country rock threw up a warmth and glare that made them squint.

There were three at first. Standing down, they sent their horses off behind a mass of boulders stitched together with bayonet and yucca plants. Two of them put up their hats and leaned against a rock. The third, Alec Winton, stepped into the road to cock his head off easterly toward the river country. He stood for a minute or two, listening. Coming back to the others, he took a hitch in his belt as he walked.

"Nothin' yet," he said, leaning on the rock beside them, and batting his dusty hat against his leg. "Quiet as can be out there."

The second man pulled out his revolver and opened the gate to see that all the chambers had their loads. Stone Johnson never cared if an empty rode beneath the hammer and pin or not.

Putting his gun up again, he said, "We're early. And if we wasn't, it wouldn't make no difference anyhow. I don't think that thing's run on time yet."

Alec began to put a cigarette together.

"Be just the day for it to be later than ever, too," he said, "while we're lying around this arroyo in the heat. I can think of a lot I'd rather do."

"You'll think of a whole lot more'n that with some of old Anders' money in your poke," Stone said.

Alec lit the smoke, and flicked the match away. By now the sky was altogether clear of cloud, and lay hard and blue above them. It grew hotter in the dip. A long-eared jack sat up in the shade of a rock beyond them and seemed to wonder at their waiting in the blazing sunlight. His hat tipped down to shade his face, the third man lay half asleep against the rock.

"Maybe Anders ain't bringin' any money with him, Stone," Alec said when a minute or two had passed.

"A miracle if he ain't," Stone said. "He's just done shipping all the stock he stole in the last five years. He's the only one in Lincoln County left with any stock or money—either one. I got a share of it due me."

Alec gave a glance at the rash of mountain laurel over the road. The look of it was mindful of the juniper and *piñon* farther up in the hills. Pine, too, and when he thought of pine these days he thought of a creek in a little park of aspen, lying virgin, all of itself, with a cabin and a pole corral nearby. Somewhere there ought to be a place like that, the thought went on. Ought to be a time some day, too, perhaps.

He began to wish he hadn't agreed to this idea. If it hadn't been that Stone had made a thing of it, he wouldn't have.

"Could be Anders won't be on this coach," he said to Stone.

"I had it in San Patricio he would be."

Stone took a pull at his hat, and looked at Alec. "What's the matter, Alec? You voted for it, like the rest of us." Stone smiled a little at him. "And you're the boss-man."

Alec nodded. "I know all that. I don't like a stick-up on a stagecoach, though. Fighting a cattle war is different. He stole. We stole back at him. Everybody fought each other. It's ending, though. He hurt me, too, as you well know. But we can't go on like this forever."

"We won't. This'll fix us up for life."

Alec shrugged, liking what they were about to do even less. "Maybe. Maybe not. For me, though, I don't mind letting bygones go."

"I do, goddam it," Stone said, letting fly with his boot at a rock before him on the ground. "I mind a lot. That son has got a piece of me."

"I know that, too. That's why you got my vote for this. It don't mean I got to like it, though."

Stone had nothing to say to that, and fell to nudging the rock with his boot in silence. Alec watched the shadows of the far clouds moving on the mountains, dark and changing in their patterns, many miles away. Looking at them, it came over him it was as if they had some spirit of their own which gave them leave to move as they so wished, going here or there, whichever way they might like, as was their mood. It made him wonder what it must be like to be a cloud, and to do this or that according to your inclination, instead of being bound by loyalty to a thing you'd stopped believing in.

Some of those clouds now, judging by their distance, would be shadowing the new grave of John Tunstall, his old employer. They'd be stealing over the grave of Buckshot Roberts, too, and of Dick Brewer, and McSween; and over the graves of Murphy and Dolan, leaders of the enemy faction, and who could say how many others, known and unknown? Some lay in marked earth, some in nameless canyons or on lonesome hillsides, unburied and reduced to shreds of flesh and bone where they had fought and fallen.

Upon the whole of that ruined and unhappy country those clouds could look and place their ghostly fingers and pass on.

A piece of a small cloud passed over the road, and for a moment touched him with its darkness and a hint of cold, as if it looked upon him, too, in death.

What was he doing, waiting in this road the way he was, he asked himself. What was he doing in company with men whose likes, save those of Alfredo and Pike Fortune, he'd not be seen with ordinarily? And where was the good to be found in a vendetta when the principals were dead? The Lincoln County cattle war was over. The reasons for fighting were plenty and good enough when Tunstall was alive, and so too when Murphy and Dolan could be fought, but they were all gone now; and here he was thrown in with such as Stone, and up the mountain, waiting, Roy Runbach and Clint Morgan, all of them the rag-tag end of humankind, who had no loyalty to anyone save themselves.

Nothing save the accident of lessening numbers had gathered them together, in the first place; and only the acid hate of Stone for Anders, last of the Murphy men, had set them down here in this gulch today. But what did all this have to do with the origins and causes of the feud, so long in burning? And where was the relationship between armed robbery and his feeling of personal loyalty to the memory of John Tunstall?

What was the point in anything, any more?

Alec shook his head and dropped his cigarette in the dust. Along with the heat of the arroyo, the parching of his throat made him feel like he'd spent a month in desert country.

"I hope they got a water bucket on that thing, at least," he said. "How about it, Pike? You dry? You ought to be."

Pike Fortune was the third man and the youngest, young enough to have a smooth face two days running, and when he was quiet and relaxed, like now, he looked even younger. Every time he looked at Pike in such a moment it came over Alec that the kid had no business being with them at all—he was too young to die, as he surely would in time—life held too much good in store for him. Still, he had worked for Tunstall, too, though not so long; and now, together with Alec and Alfredo, he was among the last of the Tunstall hands alive.

Coming out of his drowse, Pike screwed his eyes against the glare, and smiled.

"I could go for water, sure enough," he said. "Anything wet'd do me. Even a shot of whiskey'd do me."

Stone let go at the rock with his boot again.

"You ain't goin' to drink no more," he said to Pike. "I'll bat your ears off, if'n you do."

"Hey, it's the bear that walks like a man," Pike said and laughed.

"Just remember what I said," Stone said quietly, not looking at him. "I'll bust you good."

"Check with me first," Alec said, "if you don't mind."

Stone didn't look at Alec either. With a grunt he stepped out from the rock and shook himself all over, as an animal might do. Standing with his stumpy legs spread out, he did look something like a bear, at that, big without being tall, and not much shape, just square and solid all the way to the top of his rusty, unkempt hair. Even his face was that way, crude and hewn, and finished off in a scowl, so that a man could hardly know the thoughts behind it, except he might suspect they would be dark.

Pulling his hat down tighter, he went into the road and stood there with his head tipped sidewise, motionless. As if to hold all nature quiet to his order, he raised his hand and listened for a moment, then dropped it and shambled back to them. Stone never hurried over anything.

"Horse coming," he said, "up the road."

"Alfredo, likely," Alec said. "Coach could be comin' on behind him."

Alec began to scrooch around the rock outcrop that lay between them and the road, the others taking up in back of him.

"Damned fool ought to hit the brush," Stone said. "Looks fine havin' all that dust in the air."

"There's a breeze out there'll take it off in time," Alec said. "He knows enough to keep ahead a piece."

"He's made me wonder more'n once," Stone said and, looking around at him that time, Alec saw him scowling over the road, far off toward the Guadalupes, which shook and trembled through the heat waves of the arroyo. Once his back was up, you couldn't tell what might come out of Stone. Just now, that thing with Pike had got him eating on Alfredo. No doubt he was good and sour now, and given sourness enough, he did some crazy things.

Alec thought about that sourness a minute. Then he said, "Maybe you and me better hole up here, an' let Alfredo and Pike go cover the rear and side."

Stone kept staring at the distant mountains sullenly.

"Rather cover the rear myself," he said. "You can have the kid—I'll take Alfredo."

"All right," Alec said, and let it ride. He stood up and went around behind the rocks to get his horse and, coming back with it, he saw the man they had been listening to come pounding into the draw in a ball of dust, slow in a rain of stone and earth, and stop.

It was Alfredo, sure enough; he was laughing, as he always seemed to laugh, his round, dark face split with the whiteness of his teeth. His high sombrero lay over the back of his neck, and he spoke rapidly, without dismounting.

"She's coming now," he said. "She's coming now in only a couple of minutes."

"What's the hitch?" Alec said. "How many pulling it?"

"Horses? Oh, four, I think." Alfredo turned it over in his mind a moment. "Yes, four is right. And two men on top." He shrugged, smiling all the while. "Three, maybe four, inside."

"Outriders?" Stone asked, as if he'd like to catch the Mexican in some oversight.

Alfredo laughed again. "Oh-ho. No, nothing like that. But a shotgun, oh, yes. One of those on top."

Stone gave that another of his grunts, and went off to fetch his animal. Nobody had any more to say while he was gone.

"Come on, then, we better get on with it," Stone said when he came back. "You foller me, Alfredo."

Necking his mount around, Alfredo raised his brows at Alec, and Alec nodded.

"Go ahead," he said. "Pike'll be with me. Don't get too far down there, an' keep out of sight as long as you can." Then he raised his voice, so Stone could hear him clearly, too; he was being the boss-man now, no matter this was Stone's job.

"You hear that, Stone? Don't get anxious. They'll stop, all right. And all we want is our money from Anders—nothing else."

"I hear ya, all right," Stone said, not turning his head as he went around a dagger plant across the road. "Come on, Alfredo, we ain't got all day."

They went into the brush, and after a moment Pike came out of the rocks with his animal, too. He was pulling his old Sharps out of the saddle scabbard as Alec climbed aboard. Alec began to draw his .44, but let it drop again, as if just having it in his hand would mean its use.

"You be careful of that thing," he said to Pike. "I doubt you'll need it anyhow."

Pike laughed and rested the Sharps across the saddle bow in front of him. "If I know Stone, I will; and I'd rather be safe than sorry. What's got him all horns and rattles, anyway?"

"No more'n bein' himself, is all. He's sore at you, though, on account of your scrap in that San Patricio deadfall the other night."

"Never knew him to mind a fight before," Pike said. "He starts plenty of 'em, God knows, an' we come pitchin' in to bail his boat out more'n once."

Nodding, Alec looked away at the mountains in the west. It was strange how much they looked like velvet when the sun lay on them in a certain way. He'd sure like being in those mountains now, or in other mountains even farther off than those.

He set his hat a little firmer. "Well, just remember that Stone likes picking his own. Besides, your hassle spiked the play he was making for that girl."

He slid a glance at Pike, and Pike was smiling like a choir boy.

"For a girl, she'd take a saddle easy," Pike said.

"Some men got to take what they can get an' like it," Alec said. "That's another thing to keep in mind."

They were quiet for a time, and Alec soon could hear the hoofbeats of the hitch and the yattering turn of the wheels as the stage came nearer. The road wove and twisted through the foothills, somethimes pitching in a climb, at other times reaching down a slope—for a while it might run over a flat of level ground. Coming over it, the growing sound was sometimes loud and near at hand, and then again was muted and made quiet by rocky outcrops or by the lay of the land.

He started pulling his bandana up, feeling it strange that he should have to hide his face. He'd never hidden out behind a rag before, for anything.

"You ain't sore at me, are you, Alec?" Pike Fortune said.

Pike had edged up closer so that Alec could now see the downy fuzz along his cheeks. He thought again how Pike ought not to be with them and, coming down to it, how none of them ought to be with any other of them any more—they all ought to be going their own separate ways.

"No, I ain't sore at you," he said.

"Maybe I just like fun too much."

"No reason you shouldn't like some fun—we've had damned little of it lately. Just be careful, that's all. We're all caught in this together, and range wars have you splitting your bedroll with some peculiar people. Sometimes you got to string along with them you wouldn't care to, otherwise."

Pike nodded, pulling his own bandana up. For a moment it seemed that he might speak again, but the sound told them the coach was pulling the final grade before the dip, and there was no more time for talk. Already, there was a beginning rattle of gunfire, and Alec knew that Stone was doing just what Pike had said he would.

Somehow, he seemed always to be losing track of detail and the sequence of individual incidents when things like this developed, and he was in the road and driving his spurs before he knew his mind had said to do it. Off a hundred yards or more, the coach came yawing into sight, the driver standing up to fight the wildness of the animals, the shotgun twisted around to find the firing in the dust behind. Though he couldn't see the other two, Alec heard the shooting well enough, and knew that Stone was taking his pleasure boring the carriage with his bullets. And knowing the sourness in Stone, he only hoped he wasn't boring the people in it, too.

They were clear out into the road by then, and when the driver yelled, the shotgun swerved around to cover them. There were maybe fifty yards of open ground between them and the coach when they were seen, and a second hung in delicate balance when it seemed the driver might try ramming through; but when he saw the Sharps that Pike was holding on him, he reconsidered.

Everything changed when Pike raised up the terrible Sharps, and sighted it. The fight went out of the driver, and he leaned his weight against the bits to draw the horses down. The shotgun saw it, too, by then, and threw his weapon into the road as if it had coiled and rattled at him. The dust began to flatten out behind the coach, and looking through it, Alec saw the others coming up. As Alfredo swung to the boot to cover the crew, Alec drove his horse against the hitch, and forced them into the beginning of an arc.

CHAPTER TWO

SLEWING and tilting up on two wheels before it settled again, the carriage came up crosswise to the road in a boil of dust, and stopped—the horses rolling their eyes to the whites and bringing up gusts of air from out of their barrels that flared their nostrils when they blew. On top, with Alfredo there to cover them, the driver and shotgun had the look of men who'd give a deal to be some other place. Alec stayed with the hitch, and Pike sat off to the side with the Sharps held level over his legs. Save Alfredo on the deck, Stone was the only other one of them dismounted, but the show was his, and he now went over to the door and jerked it open.

"Anders, you come out of there!" he shouted into the coach. "You haul your gutsack out here in the open where I can see you!"

Stone stood back a little, then, for elbow room in case of trouble, but nothing happened in the coach at first. Nobody made a move, but the sound of a woman's weeping could be heard, and Alec wondered if the wrongness that he'd felt about this scheme of Stone's was shaping up. He hated to have a part in making a woman cry.

Nobody stirred the next time Stone yelled either, and it wasn't until he shouted again that a portly man of middle age appeared, dressed in tailored clothes and with a golden watch chain strung between the pockets of his flowered waistcoat. He wore a beaver hat and he was angry.

"What's the meaning of this outrage?" he demanded. "What are you ruffians doing here?"

He leaned from the doorway asking that, and Stone was so surprised that he could only look at him, at first, and blink.

"Say—" he then began, as if coming back from a long journey—"you ain't Anders."

That didn't stop the fat man. He put out his hand, as if to say he wasn't finished speaking—and that he wasn't used to interruptions, either.

"What kind of men are you to terrorize genteel ladies traveling through the country?" he asked of them all, but mostly looking at Stone.

It wasn't the way to talk to Stone, now that the latter had woken up, and hardly had the fat man finished when Stone hooked onto the waistcoat, jerked him through the doorway and slammed him up against the coach wall with an inch or so of pistol in his belly.

"Shut your trap, you windbag! I'll be askin' the questions here!"

Stone yelled that with his face held square against that of the fat man, and when the other saw what he was meant to see in it, all of the bluster left him, just as if he had been full of wind, at that. He turned as gray as the handsome clothing he was wearing, and when he put his hands up over his head, they shook.

Stone jabbed him once more against forgetfulness, and then shouted into the coach.

"Come out here in this sunlight, all of you! You'll get pale and sickly-looking sitting in that dark! Come out, or I'll come in!"

Now those inside were quick to move. A youngish woman wearing bombazine was first, and then another, older, but dressed about the same, both of them stepping down like chickens in an unfamiliar henyard. They were crying and trembling and cowered against the coach wall in a way that made Alec feel differently about the bandana he was wearing over his face. He was glad he had it now because he'd be ashamed to be without it and have them able to look at him.

Finally, there was a third, about the same age as the first, but more plainly dressed, as if she didn't come from quite so far off, or didn't hold to showy finery. Nor did she cower and weep against the coach, but stood stiffly at the side and watched Alec and the others, stonily.

Anders wasn't among these people, though, and as soon as it was certain that no others were getting down, Stone went roaring up to the door again.

"Goddam you, Anders!" he yelled. "I told you I was coming in for you, and now I am! I'm coming in there, and I'm going to skin you out!"

Putting his gun before him, Stone went slamming in, yelling and swearing all the time. Inside the coach, with the wooden walls to make an echo, he sounded even louder, and he never stopped to draw his breath until he'd gone on through the other door and came fuming around the rear. There he stopped a moment, looking back along the empty road, drooping a little at the shoulders.

"He's gone!" he said when he came back to Alec. "He slipped out of there somehow!"

"Maybe he was never aboard," Alec told him, surprised to feel the size of the relief that flooded over him.

"Goddam, I had it in San Patricio he would be!" Stone said.

"Well, a lot can happen in between. Maybe Anders missed the stage. Maybe he got drunk. And be careful of them names. It makes me nervous to hear you using names."

"Goddam, I got the straight of it," Stone said, still hanging on, like a man who'd dallied down his rope and wouldn't cut it loose.

"Don't seem like it now," Alec said.

"Sounds like you got sold a pile of cowchips," Pike called out to Stone.

"Goddam you, Pike, shut up!" Stone said.

"Here!" Alec said. "What'd I say about them names?"

"I'll use any name I please!" Stone shouted, close to boiling over now.

He stood there hot and puffing in the road, and Alec knew he was in a dangerous mood indeed, and after a moment he got down and took Stone gently by the arm.

"Come on, boy," he said. "Be best to drag it now, I'm thinkin'. It looks like we been misinformed. Could be Anders changed his plans. Could be it came over him that something of this sort might happen."

Just the mention of the possibility was cause enough for Stone to flare up all over, and he raved the whole of a minute before he quieted again.

Then he made a long and silent study of the carriage and of the people standing next to it. He had them well scared by now, all except that plain girl—she didn't seem too scared to Alec.

"I think I'll have a look inside that box," Stone said to Alec in a moment. "You can't tell—he might have let it ride alone."

Alec had been leery of this, too. When Stone got on the prod, there was nothing that he'd shy at; like a bay steer, he'd kick at anything in sight, and a lot that he could just imagine. Stone might be a little short on brains, but he was plenty long on action.

"Now, you know we can't do anything like that," Alec said. "It's bad enough this feud is overflowing on the stageline, without our blowing up the strongbox, too, on top of it."

"Goddam, Alec, if that money's in that thing, I'm goin' to have it!"

"By God, can't you watch them names? They're going to know us like their own relations soon, if you ain't careful!"

Stone paid no attention. "If it helps to find that money, I'll tear this wreck apart," he said. "Right here in the road in front of everyone! If need be, I'll burn it down!"

Stone was beginning to rant and foam. He jerked out of Alec's grip. His eyes were on the driver now and, going up to the stage, Stone stuck his pistol at the bottom of the seat, under the driver.

"I'll take that strongbox now, I think," he said and he thumbed the hammer of his pistol back. "I'm going to see if Anders' money's in it."

Hot as it was in the arroyo, Stone's revolver at his rear end made the driver look like he had stood in snow all night.

"By God, it ain't!" he said, scrabbling at the heavy box beneath his feet. "But you can look and see your ownself. There's not a thing in there but a bundle of old receipts for feed. Mr. Anders ain't got no money in that box!"

"I think you're yarnin' me," Stone said. "I think that thing's bustin' its rivets for the money Anders put in it."

"No, I swear to God there ain't no money of Mr. Anders in it," the driver said, trying to lift the box over the edge of the boot, but finding the operation hard because of the sweat that filled his hands and made the metal slippery.

"If you wasn't takin' so much time, I might believe you," Stone said. "But it looks to me you're stalling. I'll bet that box is really bulging out with Anders' money."

"No, it ain't, I swear it ain't," the driver said, while his hands got even slipperier.

"On the other hand," Stone said, forking off on another trail, "it might be as you say. It'd be clever of you to pack it somewhere else. It could go bad for you if I should find that box was just a dodge."

The driver gave up heaving on the box, and stared at Stone. Nobody had been hurt so far, but Stone had a way about him in such things as this that made it near as bad, and Alec felt uneasy, watching Stone wiggle his revolver beneath the driver's rump. Stone had long ago removed the sear from his gun hammer, and it would be bad business if his thumb should slip.

"If I was to tear this rig apart, and find it in some other place, I'd likely open a hole in you as big as the one the railroad made at Raton Pass," Stone said.

The driver's eyes got rounder. "What d'you mean?"

Stone didn't answer that directly, but he had only to rap the muzzle on the wood of the seat bottom to make the driver shake so hard the box slipped altogether out of his sweaty hands, and crashed back into the boot.

"Now, you stop all this and level with me," Stone said. "Or, by Christ, I'll level you."

The driver tried to answer him, stopped, raised his hands, dropped them, and began again. His eyes rolled in his head, and a run of spittle started down his chin.

He finally got it out. "…that man in back; name of Jonas— maybe he can help you. But, God's help or not, I sure can't—"

Stone didn't waste any words with the man in tailored clothes this time. He started counting before he even got to him, and by the time he came to four the man was sagging like a saddle blanket. Stone didn't have to prod him more than once before he got what he was after, either.

"In the rear boot," the man named Jonas said, his eyes not moving at all from Stone's revolver in his middle, "you'll find a calfskin bag. What you want is in it."

"Well," Stone said, "that's more like it now. You could've saved us all a lot of time and trouble owning up to that before."

Stone then took the pistol out of Mr. Jonas' stomach and smiled upon him, just as if they were friends now, and understood each other. His voice turned very soft and kindly when he spoke again to Mr. Jonas.

"But you was clever, wasn't you, at that? Anders, too, to send it with you, instead of bringing it his ownself." Stone shook his head and chuckled, as if it were a fine joke. "A fellow has got to sure rouse out in the early dawn to keep ahead of you two."

Stone went to the rear of the coach and started jerking at the straps that held the tarp down over the luggage boot, and Alec took another look at the women and the man. So far this wasn't going bad, but there was something about the thing that bothered him, although he couldn't yet tell what it was except that it in some way seemed related to these people.

He looked at them a little harder. They were different from him and from most folks in this country, although that plain girl wasn't near so different as the others. But a couple of years ago, you never saw such people as these, passing through Lincoln county—now that the cattle war was over, or nearly over, you saw more of them. Not only passing through, but staying on, too, quite a few of them. Not far back such women as there were wore calico and bonnets if they were Anglos, and colored skirts and white chamisas if they weren't, but everything was changing now. Now, as if a dam had busted somewhere, these Easterners were coming in dressed up in silks and lace and other things the names of which you'd never heard before. Their skin was soft and clear, and gave off a perfumed fragrance which, when you were near enough to smell it, told you there was something more to life than drudgery and hard work, dawn to dusk, and then some. He'd have liked it if his old mother could have worn a pair of those high-heeled pointed shoes before she died.

There was an air about them, too, that told him that they knew things and had done things that he might never know or do, things that, when they were imagined, made him feel somehow out of step and old of style, belonging to another time.

Take that man there, Mr. Jonas, if you chose to. Scared as he was that Stone should push a gun at him, there was still a good deal more to him than met the eye. Such a man as he would have his fingers stuck in more pies than you could name. He was the sort who looked like he might sail across the ocean, if he wished, or build a railroad like the one that had been carried on to Lamy—a man who made a study of the way a dollar rolled, and so knew how to catch it. Given his choice of ground, Mr. Jonas and his kind could likely make things hum. What bothered him, Alec came around to thinking now, was the easy way Stone seemed to smell the money out. It was a little too easy, now he pinned it down, and made him wonder if there wasn't something more to the cleverness that Stone had spoken of.

The thought of such a cleverness turned his thoughts and glance to the third of the women once again. Sure enough, she was different from the others, and cleverness and worldly knowing weren't the things you thought of when you studied her. There was a kind of strength to her, a kind of self-reliance, that wouldn't let her wring her hands and show her fears, no matter that she had them. While she couldn't hold a candle to the other two for dressiness and outward dazzle, her steadiness spoke out of certain inner qualities that took hold of him; and for a second, while he stood there in the pounding sunlight with his gun upon her and her companions, Alec wondered what it might be like to have a woman such as she appeared to be to marry, and to have a home with for as long as he might live.

Stone came back in a minute or so with the calfskin bag. It was small, of a size that a man might use on a journey of a week or so, and it was locked, too, but that didn't bother Stone. He just tore it open at the top, and upended it in the road.

"Now!" he said. "Come out you jinglin' gold!"

But no jingling gold fell out of the calfskin bag, nor any banded stacks of greenbacks, either, and when the shirts and socks and underwear quit piling up around his boots, Stone gave Jonas such a look as should have fried him where he stood.

"Well?"

"It's in there," Jonas said. "It's in the lining. You'll have to open the lining."

Jonas seemed to stand a little straighter now, and he didn't seem to be so frightened either, any more, no matter how Stone was looking at him.

"Yair?" Stone said, and he then tore out the lining, too, all in one grab, as if it were the entrails of a roasting chicken. Inside the lining was an envelope, and when he ripped that open he had some papers in his hand.

Everyone was still and watchful of him while he studied these. There were ten or a dozen of them, altogether, bound to one another with a clip, and on the top of them, a little yellow one. Catching a glimpse of it from where he stood, Alec knew the meaning of that yellow one, and he could tell that Stone did not. Only a man who couldn't read would need to stare at them as long as Stone was staring at them.

Gradually, it came over the others, too. No longer did the women tremble, and there was quiet humor on their faces. Mr. Jonas stood up straight and tall, back on his home ground now. Pike was lounging in his saddle, smiling, and Alfredo, even, who could write his name no more than he could fly, was grinning widely.

Stone quit staring at the papers, then; he looked at Alec blankly, and then at Mr. Jonas. He shook the papers in the air. He was mad again, but kind of puzzled, too.

"You call this money?" he spoke out to Jonas.

"Most emphatically, I do," said Mr. Jonas, not fearful at all, but confident again, now that he was among the things he understood. "It is a check on the Rocky Mountain Empire Bank for deposit in Mr. Anders' bank in Tularosa, in payment for all of Mr. Anders' holdings in this region. The transaction is explained in those papers. Take it, if you wish, but it has no value to you."

"You just now said that this was money," Stone said, waving the yellow paper again.

"It is, and in the amount of fifty thousand dollars, but Mr. Anders must endorse it first. He must sign it." Mr. Jonas straightened out his waistcoat, where Stone had fisted it.

"You mean this thing ain't really money till Anders puts his name on it?"

Mr. Jonas flicked some dust off his lapel. "Precisely so," he said.

"Maybe you got some idear where he is, so's he can do that for us," Stone said.

"Not in the least," said Mr. Jonas. "I am a lawyer, one of many representing the syndicate which purchased Mr. Anders' property. In this case, I am merely making delivery to his bank, a messenger, if you wish. In fact, I've never met the man."

Stone looked at the check again, the yellow paper that was money and yet not money, holding it like a bug he might have taken out of his blankets in the morning. Alec came over slowly and Stone looked up and pushed the papers at him.

"Goddam, all I want is my cow money, an' now here's all this calf slobber I never even heard of."

Alec wasn't much but fair on reading, either, but he knew enough to make some sense of what was in the papers and on the check.

"It means he sold out everything," Alec said in a moment. "Lock, stock and barrel. It likely means he's left the country, too."

"I'll be goddamned." Stone breathed it out. "How'll he get his money, then?"

"He can draw against it at the bank. He's only got to write, an' they'll send whatever he wants. Maybe he'll write some little checks, or one like this one, against it."

Stone was silent for a moment. He wasn't looking at the papers any more, but at the mountains, and Alec felt himself becoming sorry for him, and even a little for himself and for the rest of them. They'd always dealt in hard cash, with cartridges for change, and now there was this thing. Somehow he felt old again, and out of style, behind the times, the way these people made him feel. He even felt a little foolish.

He gave a gentle pull on Stone's arm.

"Come on, boss, we better mosey on. He got clean around us." He was glad now that it was over. With Anders gone, the war was ended, the feud petered out—he felt strange and light inside just to think of it. A whole new life had just now opened up to him, one that he could choose, himself.

Stone began to come along, and then he stopped. He took the yellow check from off the other papers, folded it a time or two, and tore it up.

"That won't make no difference," Alec said, like he might to a child.

"If I can't have that money, Anders ain't goin' to have it neither."

"It still don't make no difference," Alec told him. "They'll only send another."

"Yair?" Stone said. He looked at Alec, then at Jonas. "Is that so?'

"Yes, that's quite so," Mr. Jonas said. "It was wasted effort, I'm afraid."

Mr. Jonas smiled and shook his head at Stone. It was a mistake for him to do that, though, and when he knew it he turned white again and screamed. But it was then too late, for Stone had brought the barrel of his pistol up, and let the hammer fall, and Mr. Jonas' pretty waistcoat had a new and crimson flower blooming on it when he fell and straightened in the dusty road.

CHAPTER THREE

THEY rode on through the heat of the afternoon, holding the draws and canyons high above them when they could, avoiding the roads and the trails. They rode fast at first, so as to put such distance as they could between the carriage and themselves, but soon there came a time when the heat and the pitch of the grade began to wear the horses down. After that they went ahead more slowly; through the waning of the day, and then past the beginning of the trees, where all was going dark, and dusk came out of the earth like deep waters. And by the time that Alec heard the hooting of the owl, and gave a hoot of his own in answer, the earth was a solid black, with stars above it in the evening sky.

It was like Stone to have a fireplace that wouldn't draw, and so made it needful to cook their meals outside in the open air. Coming up to the cabin Alec saw the fire, small and hot, the way the Indian always made it, the log laid in so as to burn a little at a time, and evenly. Next to it, his knife more red from blood than firelight, the Indian was cutting up some ribs of Anders' beef. Beyond, in the shadows, Roy and Clint lay in their blankets, neither giving a sign of being awake until Alec dropped his saddle.

Then Clint, the one whose face could split kindling for its sharpness, rolled over and got one elbow underneath him, while he blinked his eyes.

"I thought you was doin' guard while we was gone," Alec said to him, letting his bridle and blanket fall beside the saddle.

"I was," Clint said. "It ain't ten minutes since I took a turn. Was nothin' out there then."

"Nothin' but us, no." Clint was Stone's man and Alec had never liked him because he was a money-killer.

Clint got his other elbow under him, pushing up, and still blinking in the way of a man who's had a good nap.

"I heard you. I heard you hoot-owling out there, an' the renegade hootin' back at you. I heard, all right."

"Uh-huh, the Apache. But not you. There's others can hoot, too. You'd look fine if we'd turned out to be a bunch from town."

"Well, you wasn't," Clint said, sullen now, like a dog who's done wrong and knows it, yet hates a scolding even so.

"No, but you can look for one," Alec told him while he sat and started to work his boots off.

Clint was sitting up, more wakeful now.

"Yeah?" he said. "What's eatin' on you, anyway? What's the matter?"

"Stone can tell you. He had one of his spells. How's Roy?"

"Makin' it, I guess," Clint said, though not as if his mind was on it. "The Indian's been doin' for him. Where's Stone at?"

"Comin'," Alec said, and then Alfredo and Pike came into the clearing with their saddles and blankets. They let them down and went to the fire for some of the roasted beef the renegade had fixed on lengths of green sticks, before they sat. When Stone came out of the darkness, he glanced from Clint to Alec, as if knowing there'd been talk between them.

"What'd he say?" Stone said to Clint as he dropped his gear in front of him.

"Nothin'—but that you'd say it. Where's the money?"

Stone went over for beef of his own before he answered that. Coming back again, he hunkered down and gnawed a moment, the drippings running into his whiskers where they glistened in the red light from the fire.

"They ain't no money," he said in a bite or two.

"No?" Clint said. He looked around at the others, trying to read their faces. "How come there ain't no money?"

"There ain't none, that's all," Stone said, munching and smacking his lips.

"What he means," Pike said, "is that the money is and ain't both, and especially ain't for us."

"Oh—" Clint went dark beneath his brows in a way that told a person all he'd ever have to know about Clint Morgan. "What kind of talk is that?"

"The kind that's going to get his throat cut for him some time," Stone said, but then, no matter how it pained him, a part of it was out, and so he had to tell about the check.

"Of all the goddam double-dealing dirt," Clint said when Stone had finished. "That was cheatin', if ever I heard of it. I hope you gave it to Anders good for that."

"He wasn't ridin'," Stone said, still gnawing on his beef, not looking up.

"Oh, but he gave it to the one who had the check," Alfredo said. Reaching over, he slapped Stone's leg and laughed. "He gave it to that one very good indeed."

"I've had about enough from you, too, Alfredo," Stone said. "I've had enough from all of you. It makes me sick to hear your voices."

Stone took another bite and, as he chewed it, looked at Alec.

"An' I'm especially sick of yours," he said. "All the way up here all I heard was you yappin' at me. Every foot of the way, I heard you yappin'. It made me sick enough to puke."

"Not that you didn't have it comin'," Alec said. "I never knew you could be so dumb before. Cuttin' down a man like he was. Why in hell did you have to kill him?"

"It took that smile off'n his face," Stone said. Then, as he'd finished the piece of beef, he waggled the bone at Alec and squinted. "An' I ain't so sure he didn't threaten me, too, on top of all his insults. I wouldn't be a bit surprised but what he had a hideout derringer in that vest, somewhere."

Alec shook his head. "Some ways you're like an old woman, having to get in the last word—or the last bullet. The Lincoln County war's over—you had no call to shoot."

Stone said darkly, "Maybe it wasn't the last bullet—you keep talkin'."

"I'd of shot him, too," Clint said, playing up to Stone again, now he had got over his suspicions. "Even without he threatened me. Stealin' our money is cause enough, the sonofabitch. By hell, I think I might have shot him in the guts. I had plans for that money. Big plans."

"You ain't the only one," Stone said, slinging the bone in the fire and drawing his greasy hands along his pants legs.

"I had it figured to pull for Monterey," Clint said, gazing away through the dark, his thin face lighting up with what the money could do for him in Monterey.

"I don't know why you got to go so far," Stone said. "Paso del Norte is plenty good enough for me."

"That's account you never been nowhere," Clint said. "Lemme tell you something about Monterey."

"How do you know I never been nowhere?" Stone said. "It seems to me you're takin' a lot for granted. I been plenty of places. That's how I come to settle on Paso del Norte. Down there, I can get a monte game any time I like. Any time at all."

"You think I won't in Monterey?'" Clint said. He leaned forward some. "Listen, Stone, the sun don't set on the monte games in Monterey. It just don't set, that's all. An' it's all no-limit, too."

Stone laughed and raised his hand, himself drawn into the pleasure of spending the money they didn't have.

"Why, you don't think there's any limit on the monte where I'm goin', do you? Well, there ain't—it's hot an' plenty fast. And speakin' of hot, there's girls, too—"

The thought of the girls that could be found where Stone was going made Clint put up his face and laugh so hard that all of his rotten teeth showed in his mouth.

"Why, Stone," he said, "there's girls in Monterey can kill you with their lovin', then bring you back to life! I'll have one by day, an' one by night, each."

Such girls as Clint was going to have himself in Monterey gave Stone a moment's pause and, in the quiet Alec went over to Roy, who still lay under his blanket close to Clint.

"You awake now, Roy?" he said, and nudged him with his foot.

"Yuh, now I am," Roy said, rolling over slow and looking up. He was middle-sized, with wide-apart eyes that gave him a look of trailing the talk a word or two.

"How's the head tonight? Feelin' any better?"

"Aches some now," Roy said. "Ain't bad, though, when I'm asleep. Anyhow, I don't feel nothin' then. I guess it's comin'."

Kneeling down beside Runbach, Alec spread the wrapping with his fingers to study the ragged crease that ran along the other's scalp up over his ear. He had no personal feeling about the man because Roy Runbach was a money-killer, too, like Clint, but as he felt bound to Clint and Stone, so did he feel bound to Roy, and was obliged to see to him. They were survivors of a cause that had banded them together, and though the shooting was now over, some ties remained.

"It don't look so bad now, anyway," he said.

"No, I guess it ain't. The Indian keeps fussin' with it. He keeps puttin' that stuff he makes on it."

"Yerba," someone said, and then the renegade was standing over them, coming in his secret way, his dark face blank with all its mysteries, his lank hair falling full below the band around his head.

"Uh-huh, that's what it is," Roy said. "Yerba. That's what he calls it, anyway. He goes off in the brush an' comes back with a mess of weeds an' packs that on me, an' says, 'Yerba.'"

"Yerba," the Apache said, as if he thought they might forget it if he didn't keep on saying it.

And then he went away again. All in a single, fluid motion, so it seemed, he went to the fire and squatted, raised a piece of the beef and sliced it off with a white flick of his knife. It was all so smooth and slick it set a shiver hanging up Alec's neck, although he'd seen the redskin do such things a dozen times before.

"I guess them yerbas do it, then," he said, shaking the chill out of his mind. He stood up and batted the dirt from the knees of his jeans. "Anyway, it's comin'. Travel, can you?"

"Travel? I guess so. I don't know. Are we goin' some place?"

"There's a chance of it," Alec told him.

"Hey? What d'you mean by that?" It was Stone, who, having blown away his money on the girls and monte, had come back. "How come you say we're goin' somewhere? You ain't talked to me about no travelin'."

"It's just a thought I got," Alec said, going over to sit by his gear again. "It wouldn't surprise me none but what we got visitors tonight."

"Up here?" Stone said. "On account of Jonas, you mean?"

"Uh-huh," Alec said. "On account of him."

"How come you're so goddam sure of that?" Stone demanded.

"I only said it wouldn't surprise me none."

"Ah, you're crazy," Clint said, pleased to get back at Alec. "Who'd come chasin' up here in the dark, all because of one man only? Think of all the ones that got it in the Lincoln County war; must be fifty altogether. An' who went sneakin' around at night on their account? Few an' seldom, as I remember. It's dangerous foolin' around at night; a fellow could get hurt."

Alec reached for a bottle of cool creek water and drank.

"This Jonas was no ordinary cowpoke, nor a saddle bum. He was different. He had something in back of him. A man like him is a new kind out here. Big."

He stopped, turning the bottle in his hand, trying to think how he could put it into words, this feeling that he had for Jonas—the way Jonas had dressed, his talk, the meaning of those papers and the little yellow check—how they seemed to mean a change had come out here. Maybe big was the only word to use. Yet that didn't tell it all, by any means. It only gave a hint of what might lie beyond.

"He had nice clothes," Alfredo said in the pause of Alec's thinking. "They fit him like the skin of a fish. Just so. He wore a vest that had all over it flowers, bright and almost living they looked so real. And a chain, too, between the pockets—a little gold one."

Alfredo's teeth were very white in the solid earthy roundness of his face, and he looked at Clint and laughed softly.

"*Si,* Clint, he was something to look upon. One time, long ago, when I was yet a *nino,* I knew of such a man. I was visiting some relations down in Chihuahua. Once I saw him, too. Very great *rico,* this man was. He, too, wore fine clothes, and spoke in a certain way. The raising of his left hand would begin a revolution. And when he raised his right, it was at an end." Alfredo paused again, and laughed in his silent way at Clint. "The time I saw him, he had flowers on his vest."

Nobody spoke at first and Alec could tell by the quiet that Alfredo had put it better than he because he'd brought it down to terms they knew of. Even Clint had got the drift of it, and eyed Alfredo quite a while before he spoke again.

Then he said, "Yah, so what if he got all that, them clothes, an' such, an' is big that way—it still don't mean they're comin' up tonight. And even if they was, how could they know where to look? They don't know it was this bunch—you was covered, wasn't you?"

"For all the good it did," Alec said. "Stone, though, he shot off more'n his gun down there."

"Yes," Alfredo said. "A very courteous fellow, Stone. He introduced us all."

But Stone had nothing more to say about it; he only kept his eyes upon the fire, glowering and mean, and it was hard to tell if he was now too mad to talk, or if he had gone off somewhere again to spend his money on the girls and monte games.

CHAPTER FOUR

PUTTING a cigarette together, Alec lighted it and leaned against his saddle with his legs before him, half lying and half sitting, stretching out. Save the renegade standing guard beyond the thicket, all the others were asleep or rolled up in their blankets, quiet.

But Alec couldn't bring himself to sleep just yet. He was tired, but too many things kept shifting through his mind.

He heard the night sounds, near and far, and watched the spurts of flame throw up their light and shadows. This shack and clearing were Stone's; off and on during the past few years they'd been at different ranches, sometimes staying on for days or weeks, sometimes for months, depending on how the fighting might be going at the time.

In the early days of the Lincoln County feud, when the big land-owning principals had been alive, or still in business, they'd stayed at Tunstall's spread, or one of the other big ones, and for a while in Lincoln town itself, fighting for McSween, who had taken up the feud after Tunstall had been killed.

But the killing of McSween, too, shot down with a Bible in his hands, while his house went up in flames about him and his missus pounded her piano, had brought an end to those regular payroll days. Ever since that long-gone time they had hunted work where they could find it—a week at a time, a month, a day or two, always ready to fight; and sometimes, if alone or thinly numbered, having to ride and git when they were come upon by enemies. Then, too, there were long periods of living in the hills and timber, rolling up in a blanket under a ledge or a tree, hardly daring to sleep and with weapons ready to hand, killing an Anders or a Murphy beef for food.

And now they were at Stone's a while, over south of San Patricio, and some hours into the hills from where they'd stopped the coach.

Stone's place was something, Alec often thought. In one way it was the end of everything, the last rung on the ladder, and in another way it was a joke; a gather of tilting lean-tos in a thicket by the creek, looking for all the world as if the wind might scatter it far and away whenever it so wished.

The stock was that way, too; and such animals as he'd seen at Stone's had brands on them so blotched and burned you couldn't read them. If their ears or dewlaps had been slit before, why, Stone had slit them still again, so that they hung in tatters all over the animal's head and brisket. Whenever Stone would get to raving about the way that Anders and Murphy and that crowd had robbed him blind, Alec had to laugh because he knew that Stone had scarcely a pound of honest beef, and likely never did have. And even if he did far back in some other time, Stone would put his failures and defeats upon the shoulders of another—in that way he was a natural for feuding, which gave him opportunity to work revenge on those who in his mind were in conspiracy against him.

He knew Stone now, and all about him—knew him for a small-time cowman who'd gone bad. He wasn't any joke to Alec any more. Yet, in the way that men align themselves in time of trouble, they had fought together. And no matter their ends were different, he'd come to feel for Stone a measure of the loyalty he felt for Tunstall's memory. The two things were not the same, however, and often his feelings puzzled him.

He knew the same lingering loyalty for Clint and Roy, and the Apache; though God alone knew why, for they were money-killers—Morgan and Runbach anyway, from what he'd come to know of them. And it wasn't much he knew about them either, except Dick Brewer'd paid them off a time or two when he was living, still. And Brewer'd been an old-time Tunstall man, himself, until he had been killed by Buckshot Roberts up at Blazer's Mill.

But wherever Brewer'd found them, Alec neither knew nor cared because they hung around with Stone these days, biding their time and waiting for one of his schemes to hatch. And that was enough to know.

The Indian was Stone's man, too—an Apache from the Mescalero reservation up the mountain, a renegade gone wild again. While he was meant to do the cooking and the camp work, a man had only to watch him mumble over his warbag and see him fondle those tired eagle feathers and musty scalps to know what he had on his mind.

They were a different kind, those four, different from himself and different from Alfredo and Pike Fortune, too, who like himself had fought for principle and not for pay, simply in line of work. That was the dividing line, and where the difference lay; and now he felt a sourness come over him for having let his two men stay on with him until that difference had got them into something that had nothing to do with the cattle war at all.

When he felt the cigarette grow hot against his fingers, he let it go in a little arc such as a shooting star might make in the August sky. And as the night was cooler now, he pulled his blanket over him, and saw Pike wide awake and grinning at him in the dark.

"I thought you was asleep," Alec said.

"Dozed a while, I guess," Pike said. "Then I saw your smoke, and got to wondering when you'd set yourself afire."

Alec said restlessly, "I ain't too much on sleep tonight."

"Me neither. Good night for it, too. Cool, plenty; and look at all them stars."

They watched the stars a minute, quietly. Far off, one of those crazy-looking steers of Stone's set up a bawling, then fell silent.

"You reckon they'll be coming up for sure tonight?" Pike asked in a while.

"Maybe," Alec said. "It could go either way, I guess."

"I suppose it could. But, there's a chance, I mean. I mean, like you said, he was no ordinary cowbum."

"No, he wasn't, that's sure," Alec said. "He was different, all right."

"Not only him, the women, too," Pike said, as if the nature of the people stood out more in his mind than the danger of the killing to themselves. "They were plenty different. I don't think I ever saw women of their likes out here before. They were something, the young ones, anyway."

"I kind of liked the look of them, myself," Alec said, the plain girl coming to his mind again, all at once, just the way she'd stood there by the coach wall, unafraid.

"Sort of gives a man ideas, don't you think? Just there being such women-folk as them around? I mean, if you could see enough of 'em."

Pike was smiling widely now, and looking at him. Alec felt a laugh rise up in him. He'd thought of Pike as just a kid for so long he'd nearly missed his being a male animal, too.

"It don't take more'n one to do it," Alec said, thinking of the plain girl still, seeing her hands, the straightness of her back.

"No, I guess it don't, at that."

They were quiet for a time again. Off among the trees some scampering kind of little animal was rustling in the underbrush. Over them, a night bird passed, swift and whispering. As if in pain, Stone's crazy-looking steer let out another bawl, but farther off.

"I wonder where them folks were goin', Alec," Pike said when a minute or two had passed.

"Why, they could be going almost anywhere, I guess. Maybe Lincoln town. Maybe over the Rio Bravo way. There's a lot of towns in that direction."

"I know. That's my country over there, the Rio Bravo," Pike said.

"Is that so?" Alec said. "I never knew that."

"Uh-huh," Pike said. "The Rio Grande, near Bernalillo. Alfredo comes from over that way, too, but north more. Up beyond Santa Fe, I think."

It was funny, Alec thought, how you could know a man and like him, yet have a part of him a secret unless he spoke of it. He knew Alfredo came from up the Rio Grande somewhere, but here was Pike, surprising him.

"But these people," Pike said, while he got an elbow under him to see Alec better, "there's a lot of them coming in these days, ain't there? I mean folks different from cowmen, an' the like of us. Townfolk, say, and those having in mind to do things we never thought about. Maybe set up a trade of some kind, things like that."

"Yes, that's so," and Alec felt a mild surprise that Pike should see those people in the coach the same as he, Alec did. "You ever think of such?"

"You mean about setting up a trade, like?"

"Well, not that exactly," Alec said. "I just mean taking up somewhere, permanent."

"Well, I guess I thought of it more'n once," Pike said. "But you know how it is when you're young. You got to raise hell and see the world."

"That's so. But a man ain't young forever; look at me."

"Uh-huh," Pike said. "I'm looking at you. I don't see you settin' up nowhere."

"I aim to, though, some time, when things clear up. It's you, though, we're speakin' of. What you got over there at Bernalillo, anyway? You got people there?"

"Not no more, I ain't," Pike said. "I got some land left to me, though. That's still there."

"Land?" Alec said. "What kind of land is that?"

"Well, it ain't so much, I guess. Some grazing, high up from the river, some level in the bottoms to raise hay an' such. My grandsir left it to me. He come out this way in the early days, beaver trapping, and got it on a Spanish grant. There's a fellow looking after it till I go back again."

"Sounds pretty nice to me," Alec said.

"Uh-huh," Pike said. "I guess it is. Funny, ain't it, how you come to know a thing better once you get away from it? Leavin' it, I never gave a thought to it, but it's been different lately."

Pike scooped up a handful of the dirt beside his blanket, and watched it pass through his fingers as though it were the rich earth of the Rio Bravo bottoms. There came a roundness to his voice, a sense of distance, like he had traveled over there, and stood beside it, looking at it now.

"Queer what you remember of a place. Mostly it's the little things, I guess, that stick with you, and give a meaning to it. Like the water coming into the ditches in the spring—in March it was, some time after they'd been cleaned, of course. But coming in, then, for the first time that year, all silver and blue-white with the melt, and shining in the sun. My grandsir, he'd get down and scoop a little up, an' drink of it, and then, if I was with him, he'd scoop a little up for me, and I'd drink, too. 'New life, *companero*,' was what he'd say of it. 'New life to us, and to the land.' "

Pike took up another hand of dirt and let it run down through his fingers. Alec made a cradle of his arms and let his head lay back in them; he could see Pike's grandsir standing in the sunlight, the water in his beard, his hands shaped into cups.

Pike said, "It's things like that that stay with you. The Indians, too—Pueblos over there—going through their fields to bless the crops, all in a line and holding a statue of their patron saint above them as they walked. And out in front of them the padre in a black robe, like a dark bird. Then the haying in the summer, smelling sweet and wet, and like as not a thunderstorm on the mountain to make you hurry. And in the fall the chili peppers, hanging from the vigas, in long *ristras,* red and bright. Then, as the nights turned cold again, there'd be the smell of piñon smoke." Pike laughed, letting the last of the dirt run through his fingers. "I was just a kid when those things happened, and maybe it's like a kid to remember what I do about 'em."

"No, it ain't," Alec said, feeling an ache in himself, a wanting for something he'd never had and maybe never would, the way things looked just now. "It ain't like any kid at all. It's what you ought to have. It's where you ought to be right now. You ought to marry up with some nice girl an' take her back there. You could do worse—in fact, you're doin' it."

"Maybe," Pike said. "Sometimes I don't know, though. Like I said, I got a yen to raise some hell and see things. Maybe I ain't over that. Still, I guess I thought of it, all right."

"Well, bear down some," Alec said. "Could be you ain't got much time."

"Uh-huh. Maybe so." Pike fiddled in the dirt, and let his eyes rove off in the dark. "You ain't said about yourself, Alec. You got a place somewhere, waiting for you?"

"I got no place, Pike."

"Folks, then? You got folks somewhere?"

"No, I got no folks either," Alec said.

"I guess they're gone, too, huh?" Pike said, as if he'd like to know but didn't like to ask outright and so seem to be too prying.

"That's right," Alec said. "Long ago. Comanches."

In the quiet there was a sound, or maybe it only seemed there was a sound. But there was movement in the dark, and when the movement became definite Alec saw the Apache separate from the mass of trees and come into the clearing and stop beside the fire ring. For some moments the renegade stood there like he'd taken root, his head turned toward the crowns of the trees, deep-colored and smoothly carved in the little glow that still came from the fire—then he dropped on all fours and put the side of his head against the ground.

As he stood again Alfredo threw off his blanket and went over to him. Pike got up. Alec reached over for his boots, and pulled them on before he moved. He knew how things were shaping up, and they might as well start getting ready for it.

They were all three standing with their heads tipped, listening, when Alec came over to them.

"They're comin', sure enough," Pike said. "Just like you said they might."

"How about it, Indian?" Alec said, pushing his shirt down into his jeans, and taking up on his belt.

The renegade made gestures with his arms and got on the ground again to listen.

"He speaks of horses on the way," Alfredo said. He made a gesture like the renegade had made and laughed. "Plenty horses coming here."

"Is he sure?" Alec said. He always wondered how the Indian could hear things in the ground and make out what he heard to be a certain thing.

"Oh, yes, he's sure," Alfredo said and laughed again. "Plenty sure. Plenty horses, too."

"Well, we better see to our own, then," Alec said. "The Indian better bring them in. And, Pike—you might as well gather up such food as we got left. We can't stay here."

Trying to put some plan together, Alec looked around him while he spoke—as if the dark might hold an answer if he could only recognize it. Clint was sitting up now, slowly, and Roy rolled up first on one arm, and then the other, favoring his head-hurt. Only Stone, of all of them, was still sleeping.

"How come we can't stay here no longer?" Clint said, sounding sore, in the way of a man who hears but a part of a thing and puts his back up at the sound of it.

" 'Cause they're comin'," Alec said. "The posse. You better drag it while you can."

"Yah? You been sayin' that all night."

"It ain't me said it this time," Alec said. "It's the Indian's idea. Stay if you want, though, if you don't mind hanging."

But the Indian's having said it put a different face on it, and Clint began to pull himself together in a hurry.

Alec went over to Stone and brought the flat of his boot against his buttocks.

"Come on, Stone, pile out. We got a ride comin' up, thanks to you."

Stone gave out a grunt and moved some, but settled back. Alec swung his boot again.

"Stone. Get up, Stone. Move your tail, you silly bastard. We got to hump it."

That time Stone got life in him and rolled over, mostly asleep still, but awake enough to know he was being pushed around.

"Who you kickin'?" he said, turning his head to look. "Alec? Who you kickin' an' callin' names like that?"

"It's you I'm kicking, Stone. Come on. Roll out. You brung a posse down our necks."

Stone rolled over on his belly, got his knees and arms beneath him and pushed up. Getting to his feet, he stared around him at the horses the renegade had brought in and at the men now busy with the rigging of them. Gradually his eyes came back to Alec.

"I don't like that kicking."

"Can't be helped, Stone," Alec said, kneeing the belly of his horse as he drew the latigo. "You sleep too hard. Had to wake you somehow."

"You're comin' close to sleepin' harder," Stone said quietly.

"So?" Alec said.

He let go the strap and turned. All at once it was very quiet in the clearing. As if a signal had been given, the others left off doing whatever they had been doing, and looked at Stone and Alec. Even the horses gave off making the sounds and motions that a horse will make when getting rigged—as if they, too, had a scent of something in the air and were made watchful by it. For close to half a minute the only sounds came from Runbach, who was mounted now, and lying forward on the neck of his horse, letting a groan come out of him from time to time.

Then a new sound came—a far-off rumble. It made the renegade raise his hand, and nod his head.

The sound was deep and distant in the earth, more than in the night air. They felt it in their boot soles as all their senses keened to it.

"They come," Alfredo said. "Ho—now they come for sure." He was hardly grinning now.

"Yair," Stone said, slow, and in a way that suggested he'd just now put his mind to trouble as something that could happen. "There is something comin' up, at that."

"Not that you ain't been advised there was beforehand," Alec said.

"I don't know as I got to take everything that's told to me as gospel," Stone said. "Least of all from you."

"All right, have it your way," Alec said, sensing his moment of tension with Stone was past, and knowing the others felt it, too. They turned to finishing up their rigging and getting ready to leave.

"How we going to do this, Alec?" Pike said, mounted now.

"I guess we better split some way. Roy can't stand no banging through the country in the dark."

"I don't know we got to favor anyone," Stone said, as if it were a principle with him to object, no matter that Roy was his man.

Everyone was mounted now, and waiting. The sound of riders coming in was still distant, but it was steady now, and no longer anything that needed guessing at. It held both purpose and urgency.

"Me and Stone'll draw 'em off," Alec said, ignoring Stone's niggling. "The rest of you head west. Better go up to the Mescalero and wait for us. If that Indian's good for anything he'll find a place where you can lay up till we get there."

"Maybe I better come with you," Alfredo said, bringing his horse beside of Alec's. "I don't like the way she stacks up. Many things can happen in the dark."

"I know," Alec said. "I know all that. But two can do it better than a crowd, an' so long as Stone's the one that got us into this, it's only right he helps to get us out. If he ain't afraid, that is."

"I ain't afraid of nothin'," Stone said, done with arguing, and mean and quiet once again, like he was brooding to himself.

"That's good news," Alec said. "You an' me'll wait here for 'em, then. The rest of you pull out," he told Alfredo. "We'll see you in a day or two. Better take the creek as far as you can. Should they double back by daylight, they won't find your trail so easy."

After that there was no more time for talk. The sound was close upon them now, broken into separate noises, so that you could almost count the nearing horsemen.

"Go on, git," Alec said.

"All right, we go," Alfredo said, and upon the raising of his arm, there was a creak of leather and a jingle of harness as they set to moving.

"Ride quiet as you can," Alec spoke out as they began to file past him.

Alfredo said across his shoulder, "And you ride careful."

Alec made no reply.

He watched them go across the clearing toward the creek, seeing them individually a moment, then losing them in the dark mass of the trees. The sound of their going passed quickly, too, and only Stone was noising into the sudden quiet when it ended.

Like he had brooded long enough, he had the kicking of his butt to think about again.

"I don't take to that, Alec, that kickin'," he was saying. "Ain't nobody can beat on my tail like you done, like it was some kind of drum, an' get away with it."

"Come on, Stone, I had to wake you," Alec said. "Was no time to croon you into life. I can't say you acted like you felt it much."

"That don't make no never-mind," Stone said. "I still don't cotton to it. Don't cotton to it nohow at all. You hear me, Alec?"

"I hear you all right, Stone, though I ain't really listening to you," Alec said. "But keep on yapping just the same. It's as good a way as any to draw 'em to us."

CHAPTER FIVE

FOR all the fact the coming riders now made noise enough to be on top of them, it seemed to Alec that he and Stone sat there in the clearing nigh an hour before he was convinced it was time to move. Finally the press of sound put the posse just beyond the thicket, and the horses were put to a walk, to approach the cabin carefully. "C'mon, Stone," Alec said, necking his horse around, slanting away for the creek. "They're close enough. Let's go."

"I don't know I like to be run out of here in the middle of the night," Stone said. "It's bad enough a man gets kicked from bed without he gets drove out'n his own place, too, on top of it."

"It ain't as if it couldn't have been helped, if you'd only used your head back there at the stage."

"That's got nothin' to do with not liking it," Stone said. "I got half a mind to stay right here an' make 'em pay for all this trouble."

"Stay, if you want. There can't be more'n a dozen of 'em," Alec said. "I'd give you five minutes to last against 'em, four of that to get you spotted."

"Why, Alec, I'd bet I'd go plenty longer'n that," Stone said. "A whole lot longer."

"What you goin' to bet with, Stone? You already blew your money on the girls and monte. C'mon."

"I guess I can spend it as I want to," Stone said, as if it had been real money all along, and he would stand for no one telling him what to do with it.

"Go ahead," Alec said. "It just means you got nothing left to bet with."

"Goddam, Alec, you keep twisting things around on me. I only said I would, that's all. It's the idea of the thing that counts. It's a plenty sad day a man gives up his ground without getting his price—or his fight."

But he followed Alec through the dark, down toward the creekside where rocks would give off a sound against iron shoes. The first ringing clash of hoof on stone brought a whoop and holler down upon them from the clearing.

"Them bastards!" Stone said, as if it took the yelling to make the riders real for him.

"That does it," Alec said, putting his horse to the shallow water. "Let's go—let's go!"

"I'll fix them!" Stone yelled behind him.

Alec had got up on the other side of the creek by then. Turning to see if Stone was with him, he saw the flare of Stone's revolver and heard the heavy bullet slamming through the trees.

"C'mon, you damn fool!" he shouted. "They know we're here!"

"They're goin' to know I'm here in particular!" Stone yelled.

He fired again, the blast echoing in a swell of sound along the creekside. From above came an answering burst of ragged flame and the high spang of bullets glancing off rock. Then came the sound of horses spurred to a gallop.

"Get going, Stone!" Alec yelled, putting spurs to his animal and lifting it into a run. Behind him he could hear the growing thunder of pursuit, and when he glanced across his shoulder it seemed to him he saw the posse as a dark and swelling motion shifting through the trees behind them.

Then he saw Stone, too, coming out of the creek at last, and giving a whoop as he hit the other side. And as the other came beside him on the dead run Alec saw his grin, brief and sudden, and remembered that, no matter the blackness of the moods that

Stone took on himself, he always had a furious kind of joy in him when he was pushing the odds on death.

The creek ran through a series of winding valleys to the east. From the mountains in the west, it fell away through high, cool timberlands, passing over falls and rapids in its first few miles of quick descent, young and full of beans. Below the aspen, pine and spruce of higher country, it flowed on through a land of juniper and *piñon* mottled hills, more sedate now, not giving itself to the youthful ways of its beginning, but like a man in his middle years who has learned a little how to curb his heedless ways. But by the time it reached the deep grass of the open plain below the hills, the slope of the Pecos valley, it was an aging warrior, done with battles and pleased to take it easy until the river drew it in.

It was the middle-age part of the water, that juniper and *piñon* hill-land, that they now rode, Alec and Stone, and those behind them giving chase. The creek made it valley country, long and winding toward the east. Underfoot grew short grass, which lengthened toward the water.

The hills ran up on either side. Short grass grew upon them, too, but as the trees put up a bigger claim upon the moisture trickling through the earth, there wasn't the growth of further down. The hills were darker, too, and in the night, save their outline blocked the stars, there were times when you could hardly tell them from the sky.

Holding the water on the left by some yards, Alec beat on down the winding valley toward the east, Stone beside him when the trail permitted. Off to the rear a couple of hundred yards came the hunters.

For the first mile or so beyond Stone's place there was some shooting—random, though, more to suggest that the posse meant business than to score a hit. Such bullets as came close enough to hear went wide, the only danger from them lying in chance. Alec gave no heed to these, but a couple of times Stone hunched around to fire back, as if he couldn't bear to have them shooting at him without an answer.

The firing was no more than a flurry, though, and ended soon enough, the shots dwindling off until the last echo of them was gone. After that there was a deadly silence to the pursuit, the horses' hooves muted on the soft earth and grass along the bottoms, the contour of the land masking such sounds as there were, so that at times they seemed near at hand, at others far away.

Once it seemed to Alec that they'd left pursuit so far behind he thought he ought to slow a bit, but when he looked at his landmarks he knew the distance could not have changed too much. A time or two there was a sudden nearness to the posse's hoofbeats, and fright took hold of him until he looked again and found reassurance in where they were. Then he knew the sound for a trick of the night and of the hills, which threw off a noise as an echo, or absorbed it, as seemed their whim.

In close to an hour of riding that way, running full tilt some, trotting some, they came up on a gooseneck bridging a loop in the creek, and stopped to let their horses blow. For the moment no sound came to them and there was time to rest a space.

"They're gettin' winded," Stone said. "They ain't so fresh as us, no matter we rode all afternoon."

"They're slowin' some, all right," Alec said. "They must have run from town. Still, they're comin' on, though, just the same."

"Be a good place to lay out for 'em here," Stone said, studying the lay of the land. "Surprisin' 'em, we could raise hell among 'em plenty."

"Don't start talkin' crazy again, Stone."

"How come you say that's crazy, I'd like to know?" Stone said. He looked around again, as if making sure of what he'd seen the first time. "Right here's a natural place for a bushwhack—you could hardly ask for a better place."

"That's got nothin' to do with it. It ain't our job to pick a fight, and so give off it's only the two of us they're chasing. That won't do no good. All we do is give ourselves away. I won't take no more of your senseless killings, neither. You done enough of that."

"You sure got some queer ideas of what makes sense yourself."

"Maybe," Alec said. "But they ain't no worse than yours."

"Yair?" Stone said. "What you got ahold of now?"

"We'll keep going, is all. We've led 'em off a good ways now. I almost think we can start bending 'em back toward town. They get close enough to home, they'll get to thinking of those warm beds."

Stone had nothing to say to that, and gave out only a grunt, as if he didn't think the scheme so bad, but wouldn't allow himself to say so.

"We'll follow the water a ways more, though, to get them in the mood for it."

"I'm plenty in the mood for bed myself," Stone said, as if he couldn't let any comment by all the way without making his feelings known.

"Let's get goin', then," Alec said. "The sooner the quicker, for all of us."

They went across the gooseneck, a low spread of land, not over fifty yards across, but with a different cover. The looping of the creek upon itself gave water to the earth on three sides, so that a bosky growth of cottonwood and willow and alder had set root and taken nourishment enough to cover the whole of the point in a screen of leafy trees. On the other side of it the creek again shook out its kinks and turned eastward. There the grass was short once more, the bottoms were open and clear, and the hills were easy to see.

There was a mesa, too, shouldering in from the north and setting its steep flanks down among the hills, back some from the water. The top of it was flat and ran off plateauwise a good many miles toward San Patricio and Lincoln town. Up one side of it ran an old cow trail, grooved, and tracing out the easiest grade to follow. All around the bottom of the mesa was a fringe of mountain laurel and manzanita, with juniper and *piñon* rising out of it in heavy clumps.

The mesa was something Alec had kept in mind while they were coming through the creek bed. Now all at once he tried to remember all he'd ever known about this country.

Suddenly his horse took on a freakish gait and he felt that sudden little chill you get when things go wrong some way without a clearcut reason. Pulling up in a hurry, he swung down while the animal was still in motion, hit the ground in a stumbling run. Stone came close to piling into him.

Then, righting himself, Alec had the cause of his horse's distress before Stone got turned around.

"Thrown shoe," he said, taking the hoof in his hand, running his other along the splintered horn and dropping it again, all in one motion. "Of all the times to have that happen. It must have been them rocks in the creek that knocked it loose."

"Come on," Stone said, drawing aside of Alec. "Pile on behind. Leave him be."

"Ain't no need for that," Alec said, standing now and drawing the reins back over the horse's head. "I wouldn't leave no horse of mine to a manhuntin' posse alive."

"Kill him, then, if you like," Stone said. "He won't last a mile with you on him alive, anyhow." Stone laughed, his tone allowing his pleasure at another's trouble.

"I don't aim to ride him far," Alec told him, while he mounted.

"I guess you ain't," Stone said, still of a prideful mood at catching Alec short in something. "I told you we should have laid out in that gooseneck—we couldn't find a better place."

"They're likely thinking that way, too. So it serves a purpose, all the same. I don't doubt they'll take their time in comin' through. Come on, let's go."

"Where at?" Stone said. "How long you think that animal's going to last?"

Alec set his horse in motion toward the fringe of bushy growth below the mesa, holding the limping animal to a walk.

"To Lorenzo's, if I'm careful," he told Stone across his shoulder. "He'll let me have another. We'll go up the mesa there, an' save time."

Stone looked at the mesa for a moment quietly, searching his mind for what he knew of it.

"There's an old cow trail goin' up there, ain't there?" he said, then. "Seems to me I got a memory of some such heading up on top of it."

"Uh-huh." Alec nodded. "There is, an' we're takin' it. I don't know there's been much stock over it in late years, with all the fighting, but I reckon we can find it."

"Once we take it, the posse will, too," Stone said, like he couldn't let go of having Alec in a hole. "They're bound to have among them some who know about that cowpath. How you think we're going to shake them, going up there?"

"We likely won't, altogether. Just so we keep 'em busy for a while. I don't doubt there's some among them knows about the trail, but I'm betting they won't think of it until they've gone by a ways. They'll figure we'll keep on trying to outrun them in low country."

"You're takin' a lot for granted," Stone said. "How you know the way they think?"

"I don't for sure. But I know how I think. And was I them, and saw a pair stretch out the lead some on me, I'd hardly think them in a fix. A man who's goin' good don't need to think up schemes to get tricky, he just runs it out. For all they know, we're still goin' as good as ever. The size of the break we get will go according to how long they take to find out otherwise."

"Uh," Stone said, like he was catching on slowly. "All the same, you're playin' blues, as I look at it."

"Maybe," Alec said, knowing himself the part that chance would play. "But that's because we just run out of reds and whites."

They came to the trees and underbrush—the mesa hipped high over them. Leading their horses now to avoid making a silhouette above the bushy growth, they struck off through it, looking for the cowpath. Back at the gooseneck came a sound of yelling, and even a shot or two, as if those giving chase were getting jumpy now that they were in the closeness of the bosky cover, and sought to build up their bravery by making a stir and racket.

"I told you, Alec," Stone said once. "It was a natural place to wait for 'em. Listen to 'em back there. They likely think that every tree's got one of us behind it."

"I never said it wasn't," Alec said. "Just the same, it's better they *think* we're there than for us to be there."

Stone said nothing and they went on, ducking under the low-slung branches of the juniper and *piñon* and skirting the heaviest stands of brush. Alec kept his head down, alert for cow tracks, but a part of him went on paying heed to the sound of pursuit, too. Once his boot knocked square against an old cow chip, brittle with age, and a dozen yards beyond there began to be a whole lot more of them. Finally he found many tracks all bearing on a single stretch of barren ground, going away and lifting up the body of the slope.

Their discovery of the old trail came just in time. The riders in the rear had made it through the gooseneck. There came the sound of hooves again, soft and thudding, rising to a gallop.

Stone called out, "They're comin' on again—let's go."

"No, let's sit a minute," Alec said. "When they pass, that's soon enough to start. If they don't pass, but come over here, we're better off making a stand in this brush than up that slope."

Stone gave one of his grunts to that, but had no argument and, like Alec, hunkered down among the mountain laurel, the head of his horse arched over him, and a screen of juniper between them and the bottoms. Studying Stone while he listened to the riders sweeping up the valley, it came over Alec again what a stupid fool Stone really had been to get them into this. And how meaningless and pointless the end would be should they be smelled out in this brush pile. No matter they had the mesa at their backs, they couldn't stand a siege for long, and daylight would bring an end to it, if the dark hours didn't. Thinking on it now, the disgust he felt for Stone so swelled and grew in him he came almost to the point of tasting it. And on the very edge of it a desire formed to take Stone's neck between his hands and squeeze the life from him. As if some creature other than himself had got inside him for the moment, to direct him, he could feel his fingers curl and stretch, as if to do its bidding. So real did the feeling become, and so loud the voice of its commands, it near blocked out the horses pounding by them, below.

It wasn't until Stone spoke to him a second time that he got hold of himself again.

"You deef?" Stone said. "I said they're gone."

"I heard you," Alec said, aware of sense returning to him.

"You sure don't act it," Stone said. He got off his butt, and stared at Alec like he would at something new and different.

"It ain't for you to worry how I act," Alec said. He got up slowly, feeling the tension drain from him. "Anyway, not yet."

"Yair?" Stone said. "What d'you mean by that?"

"Nothin'," Alec said, looping his reins across his arm. "Come on. Start draggin' it. Let's go."

After that they climbed. It was dark, and the trail rose erratically. There were times it was so steep you wouldn't have thought that cows had made it; other sections had gone rough and tricky from being unused so long-stretches where run-off water had been coursing down the slope and had cut through it, or where rock itself had let go, or dirt and gravel had piled up. Sometimes they had to stop to figure their way across some gully. Then there might be a time they'd have to work up-slope around a rockslide. Foot by foot, clawing and digging, some-times slipping back, but dragging up again, they kept working upward, though.

Wearing his knees against its stones, and snorting its dust out of his nose gave Alec pause to wonder how many head of cattle had gone over this trail before the Lincoln County cattle war had ruined this country, as it had ruined many of its men. Must be half a million, altogether, from the time the first one came to hunt its way to the graze on top. And like as not there'd be half a million more by now if Murphy hadn't come into the country and set the fire of the feud upon it.

It was queer how big things grew from little things, that way. Like great trees out of seeds so small you scarce could see them in your hand. You never knew from first glance at a thing which way it might develop, given time.

Take Murphy, if you cared to. If he'd only traveled home when the time came to muster out the California Column, there might still be cattle going up this trail. Or even if he'd mustered out at Craig, across the desert on the Rio Grande, instead of up the mountain at Fort Stanton. Either way, he would have stayed away from here. He wouldn't have sought to set himself up as a king among these hills and valleys. And had he not done that there would have been no feud. Nor any reasonable cause for Tunstall and McSween to range themselves against him, nor any of the others living roundabout to pick and choose among the leaders as to which held up their interests best.

All of them now dead would be alive today, and there'd never have been the hand of ruin on this land. Nor would there be the need to go skulking up this rutted path on account of such as Stone, wondering when the bullets might start flying.

He stopped. Another rockslide lay ahead—the last, though, it looked to be. Up above him, not too far, he could make out the heavy caprock of the top. Like a ledge, or roof, it stuck out over the track a ways, the earth and stone beneath it worn away by wind and water.

"What's the matter?" Stone said, like there had to be something wrong since Alec stopped.

"Nothin'. Just breathin', is all. How you goin'?"

"I'm makin' it," Stone said. "Nearin', are we? I almost think I hear 'em comin' back again."

Off to the side the sheer drop fell away so sharply it almost gave a man a fright to look at it, all black as charcoal, except against the water, where the level grass glowed palely from starlight, far off. Standing stock still, listening, Alec heard his heart pound more than anything, but the other noise was there, too, the whisper of pursuit.

"Yeah, it's them, all right," he said. "It don't make any difference, though. We got 'em by half an hour now. They still got to find the trail, and even then it won't be easier for them than us."

The last stretch was the worst of all. The slide pitched up high, the whole of it so loose and queasy underneath it seemed about to give at any second. A couple of times they set off little avalanches that slid away like grease and fell so straight and far you scare could hear them hit. One time Alec's horse went to its knees, as nearly everything solid shot out from under it.

But hardly had he got the horse to its feet again, and gone ahead a yard or two, when Alec felt the caprock under him. The ground was level, and looking up, he saw it going away into the night without a break.

Still in half a crouch, as if the climb stretched out beyond him yet, he went on some yards. Then he let his arms and legs go out from under him, and lay spread out flat upon the stony soil. From his lungs came gusts of air, and his heart was shuddering and pounding, like it might have burst out of his body if the climb had gone on much longer.

For more than a minute he lay there, scarcely feeling the press of pointed stones against him, just breathing and knowing the goodness of having made it free. Then, a little at a time, he got his knees beneath him, then his elbows, and got slowly up. Stone was on his feet already, like the bull he was, standing near his horse, and looking away toward the valley in the dark.

"They're down there," Alec heard him say. "They're down there, sure enough. The bastards. They're gathered up in a knot, deciding whether to climb this thing or not, it looks like."

"They don't make much difference now," Alec said. He hardly cared if the posse came on or not. They were just hunters, without the desperate courage of the hunted. He didn't bother to go to the edge and look, but went to his horse instead to find out how the hoof had made it.

Then, as he bent over it, he heard the sliding sound of metal over leather. Glancing up, he caught the glint of starshine on Stone's rifle barrel, which he'd drawn and laid across his saddle, while he stared down at the posse.

"Hey!" he yelled at Stone and, dropping the hoof, lunged at the other.

"Keep away from me!" Stone shouted. The stock was held against his cheek and he was glaring over the sights.

"Like hell!"

He got to Stone, reached over, took the barrel in both hands, and wrenched up. A roar and a gout of flame slammed past his face and knocked him sidewise. More by reflex than by any kind of plan, his hands held on against Stone's jerking at the stock. They both went stumbling over the rough ground, fighting for the gun, until a rock came up behind Stone, caught him at the knees, and dropped him on his tail. Letting go of the stock, he gave out a squall, and set to swearing, almost foaming at the mouth, he was so mad.

"Go on, rave," Alec told him while he levered the brass out of the gun. "I hope you landed on a dagger plant. I hope you jammed the whole thing up your tail."

"If you ain't the meanest sonofabitch I ever knew," Stone said, trying to rise, yet soothe his rear end, too. "I never in my whole life knew anyone so mean and cussed. It'd serve you right if that thing *had* hit you in the face."

"I ain't so sure you didn't try to put one there," Alec said, while the last of the brass fell free and he slapped the lever home a final time.

"I ain't either, now I think of it," Stone said. The big man was up at last, holding his rear end with both hands, like he had a fire in it. "You sure deserved a faceful. I'd have had one of them bastards, sure, except you wrecked my aim. Goddam, you had your nerve."

"I said once there wasn't goin' to be no more of them sense-less killings," Alec said. "As things stand, I guess there's no more question in their minds about where we went." He came to Stone's horse, reached up and jammed the rifle into the saddle scabbard. "You sure got a knack for gettin' us into things. Go on. Get up there. We can't waste no more time here."

Stone started in to say some dark and sullen thing, but as he hit his saddle he let out another squall, then yelled and swore.

Alec hardly listened to him. For all that he cared, Stone could shout his head off. It was better, in fact, that Stone should raise up a noise, for as long as Stone was taken up with shouting at his rear end, he wasn't apt to think of putting a bullet through Alec's back. Stone's brain could handle only so much at a time.

PART II
THE DESPERATE MEN

CHAPTER SIX

IT WAS DARK IN Lincoln town. The dark and the quiet gave a feeling of desertion, as if the town were half empty, and those not sleeping might be out somewhere, still riding the country. Coming up the Bonito bottoms slowly and carefully, Alec saw a light from time to time, but mostly the buildings were black, lumping up in solid and heavy masses in the night. Ever since the killing of McSween, this had been a Murphy town, and Alec always got a creepy feeling when he entered it. Save for Lorenzo, and another one or two, perhaps, most of those who lived here were his enemies, and would be glad to drop him if they could.

Holding the quiet grass beneath them, they went along behind the buildings rimming the town until a tree took shape ahead, a cottonwood that threw its arches high out over the creek. Its trunk was of a size to shield them from above, and they stopped behind it.

"You might as well wait here," Alec said, while he dismounted and searched the dark for Lorenzo's place. "If he's home, I won't be long."

"I don't know as I want to wait here or not," Stone said, himself again now he'd ridden another thirty minutes.

"Go where you want, then," Alec said, so sick of him he wouldn't argue with him over anything any more. "For all I care, you don't need to wait at all. Head on up to the Mescalero, if you like. It makes no nevermind to me."

"I don't know as I'll do that either," Stone said, as if whatever he did would have to be different from what Alec suggested. "Maybe I'll go up to the Torreon and sit around a spell."

"Have it your way," Alec said.

He went on foot from there. He led his horse, climbing the low bank, searching ahead for Lorenzo's corral and store. It was very dark, but after some progress such buildings as he knew began to take on shapes he recognized. Off to the right he made out Murphy's place, rising up two stories, looking lifeless—like the man who'd owned it was. Up on the second floor Billy the Kid Bonney had been kept for hanging until one day he'd got a shotgun in his hands and blown Bob Ollinger into the road below. This side of it, and closer to Alec, but not so easy to recognize for its being a flattened ruin now, lay the mouldering 'dobe walls and blackened timbers of McSween's old place. Going back to the soil, now, from which it came—though there was a moment, as Alec looked at it in passing, when it seemed to spring to life again, and there was in his mind the image of its flaming end. For a second, there, the memory was so real that he could almost feel the scorching heat. Somewhere in the background of the blaze he heard the old piano plink and clank; and in the doorway, as the fusillade roared out to cut him down, McSween appeared, quoting the words of God, walking to meet his death.

Lorenzo's was in between, standing in the open by itself, and fronting on the road. Up on the second floor Lorenzo kept a couple of rooms for travelers; below them was the store, and in the rear a room that held supplies and quarters for himself. Back a ways stood a corral where Lorenzo kept stock for sale or trade.

Alec tied up at the gate of the corral, and walked on up to the building. A light showed dimly through a window at the front, but he was shy of lights, and so went to the doorway at the rear. After he knocked there was a moment when he scared himself, wondering if those who knew of Lorenzo's liking for him had maybe smelled out such a chance as this and might be waiting for him.

But when the door swung to, it was Lorenzo stood there looking out, big and blinking, his mustachios drooping down around his mouth, his large eyes soft and liquid, like some gentle ruminant's.

"*Caray!*" Lorenzo raised a hand. "You!"

"Yuh, it's me, Lorenzo. I got troubles."

"You tell me something I don't know?" The big Mexican laughed. Then, as if Alec were a child, Lorenzo took him by the shirt in one hand and pulled him through the door. With a foot, he kicked it shut and, letting go of Alec, slammed the bar through the brackets. "Coming here!" he said. "You got plenty nerve to come to Lincoln! I ask you, does the sheep go to the wolf?"

"It ain't that I had much choice," Alec said. "My horse cast a shoe out there someplace, and I knew you was the only one who never cared about the hour when it came to trading."

"Your horse threw a shoe?" Lorenzo stared at him, then smiled and spread his hands. "How could I think your trouble was something else? Forgive me, please. In the name of the Virgin, how could I think it was you whose blood is sought tonight?"

Lorenzo laughed and gently shook his head—he could be that way sometimes. Alec took out a paper and his tobacco sack to make a cigarette.

"That bad, huh? I might have known."

"*Caray*, man, haven't you heard them howl? This man who died, you would think him the *presidente*." Lorenzo shrugged, and in the dim light coming from the other room, Alec saw the corners of his mouth go down. "But that is nothing to the loss of a shoe. Santa Maria, to lose a shoe is a calamity."

"I guess I heard 'em howlin', all right," Alec said. "They was on us pretty close for a while. Now we got 'em by an hour, maybe more."

"You don't come to town alone?"

"No, I got Stone with me. He's out there somewhere—at least, he was. I don't know if he's going to wait for me or not."

"Ho! Him. That one. You should hope he doesn't. You should hope he goes and dies somewhere. He is the one, eh? From what they say—those on the coach—I put it together, and out he comes."

Alec nodded, while he lit his smoke and took a drag.

"It was him, all right. God knows I tried to get him out of there before it happened. But it did, and now we're in for it."

"You should kill him, Alec. You should take his head off. Kill him and go away. He will be the death of you, if you do not. Be ruthless with him. He is sick in the head, that one."

"I've had plenty chances to see that lately," Alec said. "He makes me sick in the head, myself."

"Ha, you must destroy him then," Lorenzo said, and then, as if the matter had been settled and could now be put aside, he added: "A horse? Very well. I have a sorrel mare. A mare for distance, as the saying goes. You go far, *amigo*. She will take you there, or die." He took a halter off a nail. "Wait here. I will get her ready. Do not go into the other room. The women are there, those from the coach. The hub of one of the wheels was cracked, and they must wait for morning to go on. Now they wait that I may fix them beds above. They want sheets!" Lorenzo raised his eyebrows. "*Caray!*" he said, and went out.

Alec waited in the rear room, puffing on his smoke. Through the doorway from the front there came the beam of light and woman's talk, hard to hear though, from where he was. Pretty soon his curiosity took hold of him and moved him toward the inner door. There was no reason he shouldn't have a look at them, if he was careful and stayed back in the shadows. Even should they see him there, they couldn't know him—he'd been covered at the stage holdup, and the talk he'd made to Stone had been low.

They were there, all right. The two in silk were sitting on a bench before the counter. They were huddled together as if fearing the arrival of more of such fiends as inhabited this strange and ruthless land. The third, though, the plain girl who had caught his eye at the coach, was standing by the shelves, studying Lorenzo's wares. Watching her, he was aware again of all those little things he had seen in her before—the way she stood, alert but easy and relaxed. Her hair was wheat-colored, plainly fixed and gathered with a light blue ribbon at her neck. Her hands were at her waist, long fingers relaxed.

Alec drew a little on his cigarette, and the younger of the silken women put her nose in the air and sniffed.

"I smell smoke," she said.

"Barbarians," the older woman said. She put her handkerchief to her mouth. "We'll all be burned alive."

Sniffing, too, the plain girl glanced around, then settled her eyes on the door where Alec stood. Alec had his smoke behind him now, but he had not moved so fast she didn't see the passing glow of it.

"Mr. Morales, is that you?" she said.

Caught in a way he hadn't thought of, Alec argued with himself a moment. If he answered, an explanation might be asked of him. But if he didn't, the older woman might set up a squalling. It was bad enough for her to have a notion the building was on fire.

So he said, "No, it's only me—a customer. Lorenzo, he's gone out a minute. I'm waitin' for him to come back." He brought the smoke around in front where they could see it. "I guess that's what you smelled."

"Of course," the plain girl said and smiled. "There," she said to the others, craning their necks from the bench. "Mr. Morales is a trader—this man is a customer. It's only the cigarette he is smoking that you smelled."

The older woman said, straining to look, but fearful still, "What is he doing in here at this hour—how do we know he's a customer?"

"Do you often trade this late?" the plain girl asked Alec. She came closer to him now, a step or two, and he could see her even teeth and eyes. Like her dress, her eyes were gray, and gave the same impression of questioning calm and quiet.

"No—but I'm a friend of his. In an emergency, he opens up for me. I'm waiting while he rigs my horse. It's back in his corral. I didn't mean to scare you none by looking in."

"Oh, I don't think you scared us very much," she said, as if feeling she ought to put his mind at ease. "Perhaps we're just on edge a little—it's been a bad day. A man was killed on the stage this afternoon."

"Butchered!" the older woman cried, the thought of it alone enough to set her tears to flowing. "Slain in the road by uncouth brigands! Oh, it's been a horrible day!"

The plain girl asked Alec, "I suppose you heard of it?"

Alec thought a moment before answering. Suddenly he was very conscious of them, and of himself among them, and of something probing in the alertness of the plain girl, as though she were listening to something more than his answer. Though he stood in the darkened doorway, he had the feeling of a glare of light full on him. The two on the bench could scarcely see more of him than the flowing end of his smoke or the movement of his hand or arm, and the oil lamp threw the shadow of his hat across his face so that even the plain girl could see little more, though she stood nearer.

That seemed to make no difference, though. He was used to killings now, and while not hardened to them in the way of Stone and Clint, the way of things had justified them in his mind. But his awareness of these women and himself in the face of all this talk of Jonas' killing was enough to stand him naked in a beam of guilt. He almost looked to see if any of Jonas' blood was on him somewhere.

"Yes, I guess I heard of it," he said, and became aware of the peculiar exactness of his words. "I work out from here some, but I heard of it, all right."

"It was a terrible and vicious thing," the plain girl said, while her fingers worked together, as if she, too, were caught up in the memory again.

"It's been that way around here for a while," he said, knowing that, in so saying, he sought to lump it with the others that had gone before, but knowing, too, that Jonas' killing was somehow different.

"That's what we've been told," she said. "It must be a terrible way to live. And a terrible country, too."

"It was good before the trouble started."

"No law," she said, caught up in her thought, not hearing him. She ran a finger along the counter top. "No order or safety for a person's family. How can you live in such a place?"

It was a woman's view of it, and the kind of question raised by those now coming in. It wasn't the kind he'd ever ask himself in just such words, but it had a kinship with his aims and feelings and such hopes as he'd felt moving in him lately.

"It'll change," he said. "It's bound to. It's changing now, though it don't look like it much. A new place always has some kind of trouble." He paused, marking her face again, the difference he saw between her and the other two. "It takes time, is all. Maybe it was like this once where you come from."

"The Pawnees sometimes gave us trouble," she said, raising her eyes again. "And in the War there were the raiders up from Texas. I don't remember much of them, but they were bad, all right."

She spoke slowly, thoughtfully, and Alec nodded, feeling a certain gladness in his guess about her origin.

"You come from Kansas, don't you?"

"Yes, Kansas. Bad as it was, though, in those days, it was better than this."

"Yes, but you had trouble just the same," he said, aware now of wanting her to like this country, maybe not the way it was, but as it might be, given time and a chance. "Are you staying here, or going back?"

"Neither. I'd go back, if this was it. But I have an uncle on the Rio Grande I'm going to see. I don't know that I'll stay, though, if it's no different."

"It's nice there," Alec said. "There's grazing land, and land for haying, too. And in the spring the water comes in through the ditches all silvery and blue. Then there's Indians walking through the fields at certain times; they carry their patron saint to bless the crops, and they have the padre with them, too, wearing his robes and looking like a dark bird."

He stopped and laughed. He was repeating what Pike had said—he'd been carried away with it. But in a certain way the picture he drew had its own reality aside of Pike.

She smiled to his laugh, and said, "It does sound nice, but if it is, what are you doing here? Why aren't you over there yourself?"

"I might go some time," he said. But still the question jarred him and brought down upon him all the weight he'd seemed to shed a moment. It was all back on him now, the killing, the chase, the horse, the Mescalero, Stone. It was as if he had been standing briefly in warm sunlight, and now the sky had choked with cloud above him.

It was then the door swung open at his rear. Lorenzo entered, saw him and came forward. At sight of the girl he pressed his hand to his head.

"*Santa Maria!*" he hissed at Alec. "What are you doing? Holy Mother in heaven!"

The girl glanced at him sharply, but Lorenzo took a grip on Alec's arm, not looking at her.

"Come on! Come on! *Vamos!*"

"I'm comin'," Alec said, half moving, half resisting.

"So long," he said to the girl. "I hope you like it there."

"Yes, good-by," she said. Her eyes narrowed and widened as she looked at him. Something moved behind them, but before she had a chance to speak, if she were going to speak, Lorenzo dragged him toward the open door.

"God in the sky, what got into you?" Lorenzo asked when the door had closed and they were standing in the dark. "Talking to that woman! *Caray!* How many lives do you think you have?"

The sorrel mare stood waiting in the dark before them. Alec took the reins and mounted. The horse felt firm and full of life beneath him.

"I was in the dark," he said. "The best she could do was guess—an' she had no reason to."

"*Caramba,* how you talk!"

"So long, *amigo,*" Alec said, leaning over to tap Lorenzo on the shoulder. "Thanks for everything. I won't forget any of this."

"Neither forget those things I said. You know what I mean. You must finish with Stone—better, finish him! Then you must go away. Far away." Lorenzo made a vast, embracing gesture with his arms. "*Mas alla.*"

Alec smiled. "I can do worse than think of it."

Raising his hand, he turned the mare and put her toward the Torreon. In a while he could see it up ahead, high and round, a kind of tower built for shelter against Apaches in the days before they had been herded on the Mescalero. Coming around it, he found Stone was waiting for him, after all.

"Well?" Stone said. "You took time enough."

"I don't see how waitin' some on things could hurt you any," Alec said.

"Waitin' on a rope could hurt."

"Let's go, then, seein' you're in such a hurry. Come on." Setting the mare to move again, he tried to think of the words. "Come on, you uncouth brigand, you."

"Hey?" Stone said. "You tryin' to grease me up? Won't change nothing—I hate you all the same. Some day I got a feeling I'll have to kill you, Alec."

"I been told I'll have to do the same for you, Stone," Alec said.

"Yair? That'd show more guts than you've got. Who said that?"

But Alec hardly bothered to listen to Stone. The man had a meanness to him, but now like almost any other time, the more Stone talked about a thing, the less he might be apt to go to work on it. After a while Alec didn't even think about Stone any more. Going through the trees and hills, he took to thinking of the girl again. It came over him all at once that he hadn't learned her name.

CHAPTER SEVEN

THEY traveled on through what was left of the night, some three or four hours, according to Alec's reckoning, climbing and reaching out of the *piñon* into higher country, feeling the coolness grow about them. The going was slow on account of the grade, and on account of Stone's horse going nearly bug-eyed with fatigue by this time—its barrel heaving while it sucked in air in big drags. They pushed on until the darkest hour came, that time when night is deepest all around, allowing visibility for scarcely a dozen feet, and even the stars seemed weary of shining, their cold light grown feeble and old.

Then with the pursuit lost behind them, they found a place where they could throw their horses out on picket ropes and bed a while. Rolling up in his blanket on the ground, Alec heard the rustle of the needles underneath him, and the sound surprised him, though they'd been riding over them beyond an hour. Looking up, he could make out the height of dark pine that pierced the sky like Indian lance-blades. As when he had known of them the first time, he began to feel a pleasure to be among such trees again, but hardly a moment had passed before surprise and pleasure, both, were overridden by his weariness. Like the waters of a creek in summer flood, sleep sucked him in.

But almost instantly, it seemed to him, the light was again on them. First, the pearly gray of dawn, running deep with undertones of lavender—a quiet and waiting time. All the trees stood straight and dark, with hardly a sign of life to them at all, holding themselves in readiness for that moment when they might put out their shadows and try their branches in the early breeze.

Their knee joints locked in sleep, the horses stood with drooping heads and tails, as if they, too, must have the blessing of the sun to waken them. Certain wildflowers that he knew of—geraniums and shooting stars—stood by themselves in little gathers in the open spaces, holding their petals close against the time to lay them wide. Here and there a finch or jay might move among the needle clusters, or down below, a ground squirrel make a rustle.

But they were stealing, almost silent sounds, as if those that made them knew they hadn't ought to.

Then it changed. The gray gave way to silver, then to yellow-gold and orange—the light quickened and turned luminous and living. A courier of the coming day, a little puff of air moved through the trees and grass and undergrowth, stirring it to slow wakefulness. And almost at the same time, the sun poured over the rim of the world in a flood of brightness, bold and lively and putting a sparkle on all it touched. Shadows seeped up out of the earth below the trees, and reached out away from them, deep and rich. As if they had been drunk all night, a million birds, it seemed to Alec, set up a twittering and chatter all at once. Casting off the caution of the dark, there was a scurry of animal life in all the thickets. Far off in a glade, he saw a doe appear; he watched her, edging out toward browse, her fawn in trail, dappled in the sunlight.

In the full dawn they rode on again. Stone sat half asleep, still, swaying like a bag of feed. But Alec was more wakeful to the favors of the morning. Not that he wasn't tired, too; he was. But forest country made him watchful of all there was to see and hear and smell about him. It seemed to speak to him, saying things to him that Stone could never hear.

Forest country, mountain country, had always been that way with him, he now thought. Even as a kid, before he'd ever seen one, there'd been mountains lifting in his young mind.

Back there on the southern plains, where all was flat enough to see the world come to an end, the wonder of mountains plagued him. Oftentimes, before he left home to make his own way, there'd be a mountain man to stop the night or take a meal with his folks and there would always be an hour or so of yarns around the fire when they'd eaten. While pay was never asked or taken for the food and lodging of these travelers, still they gave a payment by answering his questions. Just the thought that he was sitting by some greasy-legginged man who'd stood on peaks so high they never lacked for snow, who might have camped under trees so tall as to make an eagle dizzy, would set him off. Though at that time he'd never in his life set foot on land that stood above a dunghill, or seen a tree that rose beyond a salt bush, the tales the travelers told would bring to him the feel of air as cold as ice, the smell of pine, the sound of wind among the high crowns.

Though the words came out of the hunters and the trappers, it was the mountains speaking to him for their own selves.

Though that was long years back, and in between lay a gulf of close to twenty years, they still had their say. In the old red days of the last Comanche scourgings on the plains, these mountains they now rode had been the ones to beckon him. Now, others did, others higher, farther. It was time to go, while still he could. There was nothing in this country for him any more, the mountains told him, except perhaps a grave.

After an hour they came to the edge of a long park. Here the trees were very high and widely spaced and brush had given way to grass.

No sooner had they entered it than far off at the other end they saw a movement. An Apache buck appeared. He stood very still, watching them, a glow of sun upon his white clout, and on his chest, shining like red cedar. His arms cradled a rifle; he stood as if he wanted to be seen. When he knew he had their eyes, he put his arm above his head and moved it slowly back and forth.

The camp was pitched beside raw white water tumbling down from the very peaks of the range, gathering into pools from time to time, deep and black, but rushing on again, as if going on were the only important thing.

All about it stood high pine, thick trunks copper-blotched with sun, branches dark with fists of green needles and new cones. Off in a bed of fern a stand of ivorylegged aspen set their rounded leaves to shimmer in the chanciest kind of breeze, or even if there was no breeze, like chattering women. Beyond them spread an alpine meadow where the horses grazed on young grass, eating their fill.

There were more Indians in camp. As was their way with kin—especially when said kin had found himself some Anglos to live on—all the renegade's relations had taken up with him and raised their wickiups by the water. Not only that, but the kinfolk of the kinfolk, down to distant married cousins.

Alec saw young children hardly bigger than a quail run nut-brown naked all about, their little bellies round as apples, prying into things. Girls and maidens passed the live-long day in preening, dressing the hair of one another, seeming often to have a need of passing near to Pike or Alec, arching their backs so that their young breasts showed firm and tight against their Mother Hubbards, flicking their eyes at them in secret looks.

The squaws raised up a din keeping camp, hacking away at sides of Agency-issued beef, boiling pots of squirrel or wood rat or young puppies, screeching at each other like old witches while their hair streamed down in gray strings about their heads and shoulders.

And with their womenfolk on hand to see that all their needs were met, the men were doing as they always did.

The older ones had found themselves a mudbank in the shallows of the water, so placed as to have the sun the whole of the day upon it. And there they lay, blowing up wreaths of smoke from cigarettes and pipes, nodding their heads upon the weighty problems life set on them, with the aid of mud packs, heaped so as to draw out lice.

Filling the air with dust and yelling, some of the younger men ran races with their ponies, wrestled over the ground with one another, or strutted their shiny buttocks around the wickiups.

It was these younger ones who bothered Alec most. As far as he remembered, there wasn't any exact time when they were old enough to try themselves in battle, but these had the look and sound of those who leaned that way. All of them were armed one way or another, a few with carbines or old rifles, and given drink and talk enough, they could be troublesome.

But he was bothered even more to see Stone jawing with the renegade so much, with heads together, like they were kids that had a secret.

He slept a part of the day, but he started feeling out the others in the evening when they'd eaten and were lying around the fire.

"I don't know we couldn't find a better place than this to lay up in," he said.

As he'd thought would happen, Stone picked him up right off.

"Plenty water here," Stone said. "And look at all that grass out yonder. You won't find many such meadows hereabouts this season."

"Plenty Indians, too," Alfredo said and laughed.

"You was expectin' Chinamen up here?" Clint said.

"It don't make sense to me that you complain about this," Stone said, chewing away on a bone, and looking sly at Alec from the tail of his eye. "It was your idea, comin' up here."

"So, but not to raise a townsite," Alec said. "I thought your Indian was goin' to hide us—instead, he makes a show of us."

"Ah, you know how Indians are," Stone said. "They get a notion something new's around, they're bound to see it. Just like kids. No different from kids at all."

"Uh-huh. Kids with rifles and knives and bows and arrows."

"Dammit, Alec, I can't see you cluckin' your tongue," Stone said. "They got a right to be here, ain't they? Whose reservation is this, anyhow?"

"It ain't got nothin' to do with whether they got a right or not. It's got to do with bein' smart. And it's no good havin' a bunch of armed and drinking Indians around."

"Why, Alec," Stone said in a snorting laugh, "if you don't sound just like a missionary. A purse-faced, bluenosed female missionary, at that, shying at every bush, and lookin' under your blanket, seein' if there ain't something crept into it ahead of you."

"There ain't nothin' to be scared of, Alec," Clint said, his face full of sly laughter. "It's only a family party goin' on, is all. Just a happy little gathering to give a welcome to our renegade."

"Uh-huh, the kind that does the Agent get a smell of, he'll be down here looking into it. I can't see we came up here to parade ourselves."

"I wouldn't worry about the Agent," Stone said, smiling around his bone in the way of a man who has a spare ace up his sleeve. "Time he hears about us, if he does, could be we'll be gone."

Somewhere off among the wickiups a drum set up a pounding, and in the sound of it the talk fell off, drying up like a summer shower. In a while Alec rose and went off into the trees to ease himself. Standing there among the dark shapes, he felt the drumbeat in the earth like cattle running, heavy, solid and forceful, shaking the air about him, filling the night. Looking through the trees, he could make out the dancers setting up their circle, their heads masked in black cloth, twisting through the firelight with buckskin aprons flapping at their knees, stabbing and cutting the air with wooden swords.

It was a devil dance they did, meant to ward off evil spirits and to ready the ground for something needing special notice of the heathen gods. While he couldn't think what they might have afoot, it came to him that Stone might have a notion of it. That Stone should show no care about this howling, prancing crowd meant sure as night was dark that he had something cooking.

Going back to the others, he almost felt the drums inside him. And then his mind went on again to that subtle change that had come over them all.

It was like a shadow he could see, but not grasp. He knew that such control as he'd been able to hold upon this crowd was slipping away from him. Not that he cared any more—had it been the days of the cattle war, he would have fought to make them hold the line, but now it hardly mattered.

Coming to the fire, he eased down onto his blanket and worked off his boots. Stone was staring off through the trees, watching the chanting, leaping dancers—the others were in their blankets, doing the best they could to sleep against the wild noise. Clint and Roy lay near him. Alec thought a kind of animal hunger showed naked in Stone's face.

A need rose in Alec to challenge Stone; then, as he almost spoke, Stone turned to look at him.

"I been thinkin, Alec, about Anders," Stone said almost softly.

"Anders left the country," Alec said.

"So, but not his place. That's still here. I been talking some with the Indians about it."

"Yeah?" Alec said. "What kind of talk? I've been wondering how you stood to have them thick as flies around us."

"Be a joke to burn it, wouldn't it?" Stone said. "Been a dry spring mostly. I'd bet she'd go good."

Stone laughed, but not wholly in amusement—it seemed as if part of his mind were already far away in lower country, setting the torch.

"I always thought you was a madman," Alec told him. "Now I know it. What's there to gain burning Anders' place now? You wouldn't hurt him any, that's sure. Likely, he'd never even hear about it."

"It don't make no difference if he does or don't," Stone said. "Ain't nobody going to have the use of that place any more—that's what's to gain." He glanced off through the trees. "Some of them bucks are pretty hot for doin' it."

For a second, old habits of command took hold of Alec and he said, "You're taking a lot in hand, Stone, boy."

It didn't strike Stone the way Alec intended—maybe the drums had their grip on him. He didn't turn again. All he said was, "Times change, Alec," while he kept on staring at the dancers.

Lying down and pulling his blanket over him, Alec got a glimpse of the open eyes of Alfredo and Pike on either side. He knew they'd heard what had passed, and from the looks on their faces a warning took him, surprising him.

The thought that Stone might have the means to turn these Indians to his uses made him realize that not even during the cattle war had his part of the band—Pike, Alfredo and himself—stood in greater danger.

CHAPTER EIGHT

I T WAS daylight when he awoke, with the sun well up in the trees. Blue smoke was drifting up from campfires. The smell of coffee and of roast meat drifted to him. Through the trees he could make out the Indians stirring around their wickiups, putting up their screech and racket—squaws setting pots of beef to boil, kids yelling their hunger, old men making a grumble over the early coldness of the mud.

The only quiet ones were those still lying where they'd dropped the night before, downed by tulapai.

He got up slowly, wanting to make it seem like any other day. He took his time pulling on his boots and shirt, heading for the creek to wash.

Coming back, he sat beside the fire and poured coffee into a can. Then the boiled meat brought over by the renegade from some wickiup caught his eye. He looked at it a minute while he thought. Far back in his mind a notion formed. Likely the meat was beef, but then again it might not be, and for the use that popped to mind, it could be anything. The worse the better.

Picking up a piece, he studied it. Save for Stone, still washing at the creek, they all were settled by the fire, ready to eat. Even Roy was there, pale and shaky still, but up and around now.

"Where in hell did this come from?" Alec said, setting a scowl on his face, as if he doubted the meat.

"Over there," Clint said, like it was a challenge. "The Indians fixed it."

"That's a good word for it. Where's the food we brought?"

"It's gone," Alfredo said. "Last night, I think, we ate the last of it."

"That's a good joke," Pike said. "They come crowdin' in to feed off us—now we feed on them."

"Be a better joke if it was dog meat, wouldn't it?" Alec said. He held the piece to his nose and sniffed it. He looked at Roy. "It could be dog."

Roy looked at the meat before him on the sheet of bark. All of them looked at the meat in front of them.

"How come you think it's dog meat?" Clint asked.

"I only said it could be," Alec said.

"Yah?" Clint said. "They'd think twice before they give us any dog."

"Why should they?" Alec said. "They're always eatin' it themselves. Only yesterday I saw 'em boilin' pups. Fat ones, too. We all saw that."

Everybody knew that this was so, but you could tell that none of them liked to think that it was pup in front of them. Alec threw a passing wink at Pike. He threw one at Alfredo, too, and then looked at Roy again.

"How about it, Roy? You seen 'em boilin' up them puppies, didn't you?"

"I guess they was at that. Yuh, I seen 'em fixin' pups. Still, this looks like beef."

"An' it is, dammit!" Clint said. "They was boilin' up beef, too. This is just some trick of Alec's; calling it dog without he even tastes it first!"

"Don't hardly need to," Alec said. He took a little bite. Chewing slowly, he made out the taste of beef, but with some imagination all Indian cooking could be taken for many things. He made a face and spat it out.

"If it's beef, it ain't no Anders beef," he said, "like what we're used to. I vote for dog. You're so sure I'm wrong, Clint, you taste it. Tell me what you think. I ain't seen you bitin' into it any."

"It ain't me that's makin' up no lies about it, either," Clint said, now full of that same suspicion that had made his face go black when they'd come back without the money. And not knowing what he suspected made it worse.

While he was making up his mind, Stone came up from the creek.

"What's all the damn yelling for?" Stone asked.

"Alec says this here is dog we got," Roy said, pulling his eyes away from the meat with an effort.

"Hey?" Stone said. He lowered onto his haunches at the fire. "Dog?" He put his nose into a can of coffee and took a noisy swallow.

"One of his damn tricks!" Clint said. "He knows it's beef, but he goes on sayin' dog."

"It's what my taste says, Clint," Alec told him. "An' it's more'n you can say."

"Yair?" Stone said, setting the can on the ground beside the fire. "Dog?" He put out his jaw at Alec. "Give me a hunk of it."

He took a piece and held it in his hand a moment, as though the feel of the meat could give him a clue to what it really was. He sniffed it for a couple of seconds, carefully, moving his eyes this way and that.

"Smells like beef," he said. "Some."

"Uh-huh," Alec said, watching Roy again. "Likely the flavor of the guts. They boil them little puppies guts and all."

"The hell with you, Alec," Stone said. He took a bite, chewed it with his front teeth, his eyes closed, as if to put the whole of his thoughts on the taste. Then he opened his eyes and said, "It's beef. Damn you, Alec, this here is beef. Not the best, but beef all the same. It sure tastes like beef to me. What in hell you up to anyway?"

Stone took another, bigger bite, and as if that broke the jam, Clint raised his piece of meat to his mouth and nibbled at it. Roy followed suit, but more slowly, and still doubtfully.

"It sure is beef," Stone said, munching now.

"I never doubted it," Clint said. He was chewing some, himself. "I said so all along."

Only Roy was uncommitted. Alec took another bite, chewed carefully again—then, as before, he spat it out on the ground.

"It may be beef to you," he said to Stone and Clint. "It ain't to me, though. But I was wrong about the dog. It ain't. It's rat."

It was enough. A sound came out of Roy—his eyes glazed, his mouth pursed up as if he had tasted brass. He dropped the beef and turned around. He started getting up, but changed his mind and sank to his hands and knees. The retch roared out of him.

Everybody looked at Roy.

"That does it," Alec said and stood up. "It's bad enough we got these Indians crawlin' over us, without we got to eat their dead rats, too."

"Goddam you, Alec, this is beef," Stone said, black and angry.

"It sure ain't beef to Roy. And ain't to me. I'll be damned if I'll eat more of it. I'm going out for deer. Come on along if you like, Stone—you got no brains, but your back'll do to lug one out of a canyon, do I happen to drop it there."

"Yair?" Stone said, as if things moved a little fast for him.

"Ho! I knowed it was a trick!" Clint shouted. "All this bitchin', just so's you could make us help you fill your tender belly." He waved his piece of meat at Alec. "To hell with you! Be damned if I'll be tricked!"

"Ha!" Stone said, drawn off along the new trail altogether now. "So that's it. You ain't usin' me for no pack mule either! Nor do you get me puffin' and scrabblin' up no canyons either. I'm sittin'. I don't mind this meat nohow."

"Eat your rats, then," Alec said, knowing he had his plan moving now. "They ain't for me. How about you, Pike? You want to get the horses? You might as well come, too, Alfredo; maybe we can bring in more'n one. It ain't as if these dog and rat men deserve a share of it to eat, though."

Now he had things moving, he had to keep them moving. Catching Stone off-balance might be one thing, but keeping him off-stride was something else. No sooner did Pike trot off to bring the horses in than Alec got Alfredo started on the gear. All the while he loaded up his rifle, he kept a running chatter going on the doubtful nature of the meat, the all-night racket of the Indians, the tasty succulence of spring-fresh fawn. So that Stone's suspicions might be blunted, Alec rolled up his blanket and tossed it under a tree.

"Don't let no Indian fill that with his fleas," he said.

It wasn't until they had the horses rigged that Stone broke through the thicket of his doubts, and came out into the open. By then you could scarcely see his eyes for the blackness of his scowl.

"What you up to, Alec?" he said. "There's a smell about this."

"It's the meat you smell, Stone," Alec said, mounting and sitting with his rifle laid across his thighs. "I knew it'd reach you sooner or later."

He looked around at Pike and Alfredo. "Ready? Let's go." He nudged the sorrel mare.

"Hey!" Stone shouted as they started moving.

Alec gave no sign he knew that Stone was getting excited. "Do you want fresh meat, keep the fire going," he said. "With any luck, we'll have it in an hour."

He put spurs to his horse. Pike and Alfredo moved their mounts with him. Stone and Clint stood trapped in their surprise and indecision, perhaps sensing for the first time that there was a split in the band. They watched the trio ride out.

As Alec, Pike and Alfredo rode by the wickiups, some of the bucks gave off their nonsense and stood quietly, watching, as if they, too, felt the split in the ranks of people they had come to regard as hosts. Ahead stretched an alley of timber, leaving the trio's backs exposed. Alec felt his spine go rigid.

"Go easy," he told his companions. "Won't pay us none to rush."

"*Caray,* I feel a cold wind on my neck," Alfredo said. "I feel her blowing plenty strong."

"She don't blow on you alone."

"I don't feel no wind," Pike said. He glanced at Alec and Alfredo. "Neither was that meat so awful bad—didn't taste like rat to me, not that I ever ate any rat I know of."

"Ho," Alfredo said, "there's rat aplenty back of us. *Mucho raton.*"

Alec rode on stiffly, his eyes ahead, fighting the urge to look around and see if there were rifles bearing on their backs. The alley began to narrow—the trees came close about them. He was very conscious of those trees, the bark, the bushy needle clusters. He saw cones on the dark earth, rich in humus. Jaybirds scolded at their passage. He drew a deep breath, and as he slowly let it out, the trees had grouped behind them.

Glancing around at last, he say Alfredo watching him with a small smile.

"Ho," Alfredo said. "We made it—I perspire. You think they trail us?"

"Maybe," Alec said. "Ride easy, though—sound travels, even in these trees." He grinned at Pike, suddenly coming alive inside. "How you feel, kid?"

"Hungry," Pike said. "Pulling a man away from chuck the way you did—I think you two put up a joke on me."

"It ain't no joke to be alive, Pike," Alec said.

CHAPTER NINE

"DO YOU reckon the Carrizozo Road's far off?" Pike asked. "I don't know as I've been up this high before."

Alec looked at the dense woods about them. They were passing under the peak of the mountain, but the trees blocked their view of it, so the top hardly counted as a landmark. Around them were only shadows, but in their own way these were helpful enough—they told of time and direction.

"I ain't been this high either, Pike," Alec said after a moment. "I don't figure the road can be too far, though. Three, four hours, maybe, goin' easy. We can't hardly miss it the way we're traveling."

"Let the road come to us," Alfredo said. "Why should we worry about it?"

"I ain't worried none," Pike said. "I never said it worried me—I'm just curious, is all."

"*Pues,* then let the road concern himself. Let him be the one to see that he receives us. Such things no longer bother me."

Alfredo was grinning widely. He rode free and easy, his boots loose of his stirrups, his hat dropped over his neck, his shoulders swinging with the smallest motion of his horse.

Pike and Alec looked askance at him, and as if it were a signal, they all broke into laughter. Their horses pranced and twitched their ears; their mirth had a quality not lately heard in this gun-trodden land. Even Alec had trouble defining it later—it held a freedom and a certain broad challenge.

"Hey, man," Alfredo said in a pause for breath. "Let me tell you something. One time I was in the *juzgado* over in Mesilla

Valley. Oh, it was long ago. I no longer remember when it was. Or why. Perhaps I took some little thing. Perhaps it was a fight—this lacks importance. You know, when you are young you do things. But I remember the *juzgado*. And the *escorpiones*. Such monsters! As big as rats, they were. And there were rats, too. And the stink, *caray!* My own stink. I never knew I had it in me to smell like that, but it was so. All day and all night I sat up on a wooden plank in the middle of that stink, avoiding the *escorpiones* and rats. For a month they kept me there. At first I thought I would die. Then I prayed that I would. In the early morning I could hear the burros jingling by with firewood—the *lenadores*. In the evening I could hear young *gallos* serenading the *senoritas;* and I saw none of it, neither the burros nor the *senoritas*. How painful! It was all dark in there—not a window in it, only at the very top a little slit. Oh, the crime of it!"

Alfredo raised his hand and brought it down against his jeans. He laughed, looking from one to the other, enjoying himself.

"You know what I did when they let me out? Listen, I was blind for ten minutes. Then I got on my knees and kissed the earth—yes, the earth. I kissed the air. Then I stood on my feet and blew kisses at the sun. After that I just breathed. For a whole day it was enough to breathe, just to breathe the clean air without any stink in it. I walked all over the town, breathing in different parts of it. Never the same air twice. Deep, deep. Like this. Just like this."

Alfredo breathed for them, showing the way of his breathing in Mesilla Valley. Over his belt, his chest swelled out and grew. His eyes stood out and cords drew rigid in his neck. Then he let air out in a gust and laughed.

"Like that," he said. "Like that I breathed when I was free of the *juzgado*. It smelled good, I can tell you." He leaned over and reached to slap Alec's leg. "It smells like that now."

Alec drew a deep breath himself, savoring the air as if he were an animal of the forest, sorting out each noseful for the tidings it might bring him—danger, food, or a female of his kind. It was a new thing to think of bedding down at night without first making sure you knew the ground, holding your horse to close picket, or having your weapons ready—to go to sleep in a place of your own, perhaps, somewhere, shed of worry.

Hope opened like a window before him—he could look through it and beyond, and glimpse a whole new kind of life beginning for him.

Still and all, the old things didn't die so easy either, and like a bad habit, the memory of Stone kept needling at his thoughts.

"I wonder when he's goin' down," he said in a while almost to himself, giving voice to a thought without intending to.

"Who?" Pike asked.

"Stone and them Indians of his. Wanting to burn Anders' old spread. I was just wondering when he was going to pull it off."

"You think he really will?" Pike asked. "He's always got an eye to makin' something out of a thing. What's there to make out of that? There ain't even a single head of beef he can run off."

"That don't make no difference," Alec said. "Not any more, it don't." For a second he could visualize Stone in his mind, the look of an animal in his face, hungering for blood. "He's gone full outlaw, I'm thinkin'."

"Let him," Alfredo said, laughing. "I allow him to. I let him do whatever he wishes. Why not?" He waved his hand, as though to brush Stone out of his life and away. "And as I grant him that, I dismiss him from my thoughts. I no longer care. Who does?"

"I was just wonderin'," Alec said. "That's all. Does he plan to put them Indians to his uses, he can't afford to wait too long. Hanging around, Injuns cool off."

"Let them also be according to their likes," Alfredo said. "Hot or cold, whatever pleases them. I no longer care about them either." He took from his pocket a dark *cigarro* and put it into his mouth. "Listen, *amigo,* you come with me. I will take you into the mountains in the Rio Arriba. There you will forget all these calamities, and grow old and fat in contentment. My woman will feed you up so that you will never care to leave. There you can sit in the sun at your ease, and your old age will be full of pleasant memories."

"I don't see why you think the upper river is the only place in the world for that," Pike said, leaning over and scowling at Alfredo. "You can get just as old and fat in the Rio Abajo as up where you are. You can get fatter on account the growing season's longer."

"Ah, no, *amigo*," Alfredo said while he lit the end of his cigar. "You have it wrong. The longer the season, the harder the work, and in the summer that means sweat." He blew out a puff of smoke. "During August in the Rio Abajo, I have seen the *acequias* running with perspiration."

"Why, that's a bare-faced lie!" Pike said. "I never in my whole life seen anything like that. Why, you're makin' all that up. You're makin' it up so's you can hog things to yourself."

Alfredo laughed.

"*Amigo*, come, you do me wrong."

"Not much. Everybody on the Rio Grande knows the Rio Arriba country's stiff with winter six months out'n the year."

"I most humbly beg your pardon, *señor*," Alfredo said. "That is not the case. In the Rio Arriba, the air is noted for its invigorating quality. It is not a question of being stiff."

"It ain't? Ha! Listen, Alec, you know why them in the Rio Arriba's got such dark skin? They like you to think it's on account of their Spanish blood. But it ain't at all. It's because their blood's froze solid, that's really why!"

"In the Rio Abajo, then," Alfredo said, "the cause of it must be that the blood is boiling."

"What?" Pike said. "That's another of your barefaced lies!"

"In the Rio Abajo," Alfredo said, "there is the danger of melting into the very earth."

"Oh?" Pike said. "In the Rio Arriba, most everyone's got one leg shorter than the other, on account of skirtin' around them hills. Only reason you walk level is that you been out of it so long."

It was a pleasure that his *companeros* should argue the merits of their countries to him—Alec was so taken with listening that when at last he had an awareness of the jaybirds he knew that he'd been hearing them for some time. The sound of them was far off in the rear, but not so far they didn't speak a warning, and he put up his hand. Drawing to a halt, the others gave off their talk a moment, while they listened.

The jays were there, all right, some distance back, and full of chatter.

"Maybe an animal stirring them up," Pike suggested when a moment or two had passed.

"Could be," Alec said. He listened a little longer.

"Maybe we have grown a tail," Alfredo said.

"Could be that, too," Alec said.

And since that was the worst possibility, it probably was true. It would be chancy to assume that they had gotten away from Stone without his being curious as to what they really were up to. As if the sun had gone behind a cloud, the pleasure of the past moments left Alec, setting him back in the same old rut. It was as if he'd walked through mud to clear ground, and then looked down to see the mud still sticking to his feet.

He looked around, feeling an ugliness come over him. Up ahead he could see a cluster of rocks rising to a good height. There was fern and other growth around its base, but the top of it would give a view, as well as cover. Another squalling of the blue jays, now nearer, decided him.

"Do we need to fight, we can anyway choose our ground," he said. "How do you like the look of yonder rocks?"

"Why not?" Alfredo said. "We could do worse, and I see nothing better."

"All right, then."

They rode on another fifty yards. Dismounting, they led their horses to the rear of the outcropping and tied them in a clump of jackpines. There they would be shielded from such fire as there might be, and the rocks, together with the brush around them, would soften the sounds of their presence.

"You better get up on top, Pike," Alec said while they took their rifles down and checked the loads. "Me an' Alfredo can split around the bottom here."

"You want me to holler when I see 'em?" Pike said. "Given it's Stone an' them, I mean?"

"No, don't make no noise. I'll try keeping an eye on you. If it's them, you can give me the numbers on your fingers. You know—two, three, whatever. If it's the whole damned crowd, wiggle all of them."

Pike nodded, running a hand along his jeans, as if his palm might be sweating. "All right. Keep where I can see you, though. Do you get out of sight, I'll toss a stone."

"That'll work. Get up there now."

Pike went off, easing through the low growth toward a footing in the steep face. Alfredo took himself to one side of the rock cluster and settled down in partial cover, a little pile of shells in front of him, just in case.

Alec spotted himself where he could watch their backtrail.

He waited, leaning on the rock. He held his rifle in both hands, the hammer at half cock beneath his thumb. Above him, when he glanced that way, he could see Pike high on the broken crest.

He kept watching Pike, watching the trail and listening to the jaybirds. Whatever was bothering them was nearer now, though all he still could see were the silent shapes of trees and stones, with bolts of sunlight breaking through them. And all of it was motionless.

The only way to tell was to keep his eyes on Pike. In the sunlight coming through the trees, Pike's face looked very young, boyish—almost at the edge of childhood. It gave Alec a peculiar feeling, something close to guilt to see him so. Why had they waited this long to split with Stone? Why hadn't he got them all away before there had to be a fight?

Up on the rock above him, Pike leaned forward slightly. The jaybirds sounded very near. Alec opened and closed his hand about the trigger guard and lever. They felt wet and slippery to the touch. His mind came to Stone again and he felt the ugliness swell up in him, and grow.

I hope it is Stone coming, he thought now, suddenly wanting it to be. As good a time as any to get it over and done with—now, here in this forest—once and for all. I should have killed him long ago, the thought went on. Long before this ever happened. Before Jonas had been killed. Lorenzo knew. In the way of one who was not involved, and so could see things clearly, Lorenzo had known.

Up on the rock, Pike made a fist of his hand and moved it forward, holding it ready to signal. Alec stared at it, listening and waiting. The trail was very quiet now, as if whoever was coming had scented quarry, and now came on so carefully and slowly that the jays no longer felt they had to warn of intrusion.

He watched Pike's fisted hand, scarcely daring to blink. In the driving sunlight, it seemed white and swollen. The dry air made his eyes smart. An ant crept into his collar and made burning tracks across his shoulder. The ugliness welled up in him like dark waters in a sulphur spring, hot and stinging.

That they should have to sit like this, in hiding. That even now they'd made the break, Stone still dogged him. His throat and mouth filled up with every foul and vile name he could think of for Stone and for their evil situation.

The curses were almost on the point of pouring out of him when Pike's hand moved again. Alec stared and felt his heartbeat rise. The hand hung poised a second or two, as if awaiting a final confirmation—then it opened, and one finger went up, very slowly. At the same time there was a movement on the trail and through the trees a figure came, leading his horse, bending, searching for tracks.

It was Clint. Alec almost broke out laughing.

Clint came on, bent over studying the trail, stopping, going on, leading his horse. When he came to where some sign led to the rock outcropping, he came suddenly erect. He stood rooted, staring at the rocks, then looked around, turning his head in a slow arc while his face went sharp as a knife with the thoughts behind it.

Almost at the moment Clint knew he had walked into something, there was a sound. It was Alfredo standing up. He was the nearest, and he laughed and stepped out into the track. In the second it took him to do this, Clint had drawn himself together like a spring, but Alfredo's rifle loosened him.

"*Hola,* Clint," Alfredo said. "What are you doing here? I nearly shot you for a doe. Yes, a fine doe."

"Well, I ain't," Clint said, sounding to be of two minds about Alfredo's rifle. "So point that thing some other place. That's a fine way to meet a friend."

"Well, you know, I must be sure," Alfredo said, smiling, still holding the rifle on Clint. "Perhaps you are a little buck, eh? Are you in the velvet, friend?"

"More like a spikehorn, I'd guess," Pike said as he made his way down the face of the rock to the ground.

Alec leaned his rifle on the rock and walked over to the others. "Could be he's no deer at all," he said. "May be only a common polecat."

Clint looked from one to the other of them as they came and grouped around him; he licked his lips, while his hard little eyes flicked here and there. Then he shrugged his shoulders.

"I come to see how the hunting might be going, that's all," he said. "I was thinkin' to help you, after all, given I could find you."

"How fine," Alfredo said. "Such purity of heart. Like that of a child. A little *nino*."

"You was serious, that's sure," Pike said. "I never saw a man scout a trail the way you did. You had your nose nigh into the ground."

"I was aimin' to help, that's all. You'd hardly gone before I knew it was the right thing. You was right about that meat they give us—it stunk."

He stopped, looking from one to the other to see how he was making out. Coming to Alec, his eyes held for a second, but slid off. Plain as day he was lying, and knew that they knew it, too.

"You always was a sneak, Clint," Alec said. He was getting tired of this nonsense now. The ugliness he felt came down upon him, black and blinding, like the hood pulled over the head of a man about to hang.

As if what he felt showed in Alec's face, Clint's eyes grew wider. "Alec, it's the truth," he said. He stepped back, coming against his horse. "God's truth." He began to raise his hand.

He wasn't quick enough about it, though. Alec's hand came over first. It was his left, and gripped itself about Clint's throat. His right dropped to the butt of Clint's revolver, jerked it out of the scabbard and slung it into the brush. The air ripped in and out of Clint with a sound of tearing cloth.

Now with both hands on Clint's throat, Alec watched Clint's eyes bug out. Soon they seemed oversize for such a face as Clint had; the little red veins glowed in the yellowed white, pupils blind and staring, seeming to have a view of everything and nothing. He noted with interest that Clint's eyes were brown; he'd never noticed that before.

Clint's hands were not hands any more, but claws, such as a bird of prey might have. A part of his tongue was pushing its way between his stained and dark teeth. His lips were ripped apart, and his thin cheeks were blotched with color.

He went down a little at a time. One knee gave, then the other followed. By turns he went loose and rigid as Alec bent him to the earth. One leg turned double under him, the other skewered to the side, jerking. His eyeballs started rolling upward, glinting and blank.

Bending over him, Alec bore him down, hardly aware that he was doing it. It was like the time when he and Stone had waited out the passing of the men from Lincoln town, lying beneath the mountain laurel in the dark, and he had felt the animal violence take over his controls.

Clint's chest heaved and shuddered under him.

"Goin' to burn out Anders, are you, Clint?" He was surprised to hear himself talk—it was almost as if a beast had spoken.

Clint's eyes tried to find him, rolling. Blood ran out on his tongue and flecked his rigid lips.

"When?" Alec said, still outside himself, doing the bidding of the stranger in him.

He let up a little on Clint's throat. Air tore into Clint like thunder filling the vacuum of a stroke of lightning.

"When?" Alec said.

The breath shot out of Clint in a spray of blood. He drew air in again, flipping and flopping with the life that filled him in a surge. Awareness came to his eyes and left again, as they went knowing and blank.

"When?" Alec said again.

This time Clint's eyes found him. He gagged, worked his lips, and ran his tongue out, bloody and bubbly.

"Christ—" he said in a red froth. "Tonight—Jesus God, tonight—"

He gagged again; his eyelids flapped, and when he opened them again his eyes so swarmed with terror that Alec felt a dirtiness all over him for seeing it—as if he'd seen some part of Clint he had no right to see, that nobody had a right to see. The realization jarred the savagery out of him. The blackness of his mood cleared off. He let go of Clint's throat altogether and straightened.

Clint lay on his back a long while, his arms and legs at all angles. He gulped and chewed the air like he could never get enough; he put his hands to his face and made a sobbing sound. Then, so slowly that it seemed to take all day, he put out his legs, one at a time; gradually, he got over on his belly. His motions were very slow; no part of him seemed to work together with another, each limb moving of its own mind.

"*Caray!*" Alfredo said. "He is like a deer, at that—an injured one." He thumbed the hammer of his rifle back. "It would be a kindness to kill him."

Clint screamed. Taking hold of a foreleg of his horse, he started pulling himself up. Reaching down, Alec jerked him to his feet. Putting a shoulder under him, he heaved Clint up to the saddle, where he clung with both arms. Then, as if the touch of Clint had sullied him, Alec stepped back, wiping his hands along his jeans.

"Get out," he said then. "Get out of here, Clint. Do I see you again, I'll kill you dead for sure."

It was hard to tell if Clint knew what was being said to him or not. He leaned forward on his saddle, clutching the horn. Bloody saliva hung in thin ropes from his mouth.

"And you can tell the same to Stone. I should have killed him long ago. Do we ever cross again, though, there'll be no question. You tell him that."

Clint opened and closed his eyes, their focus coming and going. For a moment he looked about to speak, or try to, but he gave it up. It was as if his lungs had set themselves to hold all the air he could breathe, and wouldn't allow it to be put to other uses.

"Now, you can git," Alec said. He took the reins of Clint's horse, turned it and stepped aside. Clint seemed hardly to know that he was meant to leave, for he made no move to get started. It took a slap on the horse's rump from Pike to put it into motion on the backtrail.

The horse went slowly through the sun and shadow, through the high trees. They watched it for a long while, seeing it grow small, seeing the colors and the shading of the forest take it in.

Then they went to get their own mounts. They rode on; but their mood was different now. Clint had changed it with his coming. In some peculiar way, he had spoiled their pleasure in the day.

CHAPTER TEN

ALL MORNING they rode north and west, taking their time to pick the easiest grades, the best ground to make their way through thickets and around obstructions; riding silently mostly, each in his private thoughts. When they talked, it was to give a warning of some trail trouble ahead. There was no more banter on the faults and virtues of the Rio Abajo or the Rio Arriba, and no more *juzgado* talk.

In the sky the sun stood higher now, nearing noon. The shadows of the trees had ceased their reaching and had drawn inward, as if wearied, gathering in to rest. It was getting to be the quiet hours, the time when animals sought their thickets, done with business of the morning. Birds left off their skitter and chatter, too. Even the air was quiet, the forest barely breathing.

It was during this quiet time that they rounded the shoulder of the mountain, and stood out on an open slope, half a world beneath them, blue-green, the hills and ridges flowing into one another and away.

"There it is," Alec said, putting his arm out toward the pass that climbed and turned among the tree-furred hills below.

"The Carrizozo Road?" Pike said.

"Yuh, it's down there somewhere. Ought to be, leastwise. The only one I know of right around here, that pass."

Tipping his head, Alfredo took a measure of the sun, and of the way the shadows pooled beneath the trees in back of them.

"Well, the time is right, at least," he said. "We have come four hours, I think."

"That must be it, all right, then," Pike said. He was gazing off and smiling. It was as though he saw the pass, and yet beyond it, too, far and away across the hills and desert to the Rio Grande. Perhaps the fields he'd spoken of were in his sight, the Indians with their patron saint behind the padre, and the thunderstorms at haying time. Alec watched him, feeling sad and happy, both.

"What're we waitin' for?" Pike said. "Come on, let's go."

Full of an eagerness for home, he looked around and grinned. Then he clucked his horse ahead a little, up to the lip of the grade, Alfredo taking up behind him. Only Alec sat unmoving; and when they knew he wasn't following them, they looked around.

"Come on," Pike said. "Let's go, let's go." He laughed. "You can see as good moving as standing still."

"I know that," Alec said. "Go ahead."

"Oh-ho," Alfredo said, his eyes becoming narrow as he studied Alec's face and noted what he saw there. "The wind is shifting, eh?"

"Uh-huh. I guess it is." Alec cuffed at his chin. "I just now noticed it somehow. You go on ahead, though. Could be I'll catch up with you."

"You ain't comin'?" Pike said. "You mean you're goin' to stay here?" He put his eyes in a squint at Alec. "What you going to do? You're up to something, hang it. You goin' down to Anders?"

Alec nodded, while they looked at him. It was strange that his intentions should be known and spoken out on by another before he voiced them himself. But Pike's words sharpened his thoughts and put a definite shape to them. All the morning he'd been riding with them, turning them and looking at them, trying to put them in a clear light. Now he had them sorted out, and the clearest thing he knew was his relationship to Stone. He'd been thinking of Stone as something he could leave behind, once he'd put his mind to it. But he was wrong. Stone was no bad habit a man could drop whenever he wished—the other was a disease.

He nodded again. "Yes, I'm goin' there," he said.

By the look of him, Pike had a time believing it.

"You mean you're goin' down there to fight Stone, an' all them Indians he's got with him?" he said.

Alec kept on nodding—it was as though he might come undecided otherwise. "I don't know if it'll come to a fight or not—or that any good'll come of it if it does. Still, I'm goin'."

"Well," Alfredo said. He smiled and put his hands together on his pommel. "Very good—yes, very fine. All of that—" he waved his hand to indicate their travel from the camp, all the dangers passed—"and it comes to this."

"I know," Alec said. "It don't make much sense. I can't help it, though. I can't go off without I go there first."

Like he was trying to see in back of Alec's face, Pike watched him with his squint.

"You're crazy, Alec. As crazy as a pony loose in loco weed." He leaned forward some. "You're as crazy as Stone, himself."

"That could be," Alec said. "Maybe it's on account of he graveled me so long, maybe because we run together all this time. Could be some of him rubbed off on me."

Pike sat straight again. He threw his arms back, and his voice went higher.

"But why? Tell me why! Ain't we shed of all this trouble now? Ain't we free to go? If we ain't, why'd we leave at all?" He let his arms come down, and looked away, through the pass and off toward the Rio Grande. "What about our own places, Alec?"

"You're free, Pike," Alec said. "You keep movin' on—I want you to. It's only me that ain't. I thought I was, but now I know I ain't. There'll be no peace for me until I finish Stone—except it goes the other way."

Alfredo, too, gazed outward through the pass a moment. He shook his head, and then, slowly heaving his shoulders in a shrug, he necked his horse away from the head of the slope.

He laughed softly, wagging his head at Alec. "This I must be sure to see. Such a wonder. A man would be a fool to miss it."

"I ain't askin' you to stay, Alfredo," Alec said. "Matter of fact, I'd rather you didn't. You go on along with Pike."

"No, I stay," Alfredo said, his way decided. "In the beginning I was here, so I will see the end of it. It will be something to tell my grandchildren."

It was a little longer before Pike turned. Then, slowly, and with his face still westward, he necked his animal about.

Alec stopped him.

"Go on," he said. "You keep headin' out, Pike."

"You don't want me comin' with you?"

Alec shook his head. "No need to. It's a personal thing with me an' Stone. Does he do what he plans to down at Anders' old place my name gets in it, too, on account of heading up the bunch so long. It's all the same if I'm there or not—so I'm better off to stop it, if I can. That don't mean you got to be there, though."

"How come Alfredo's goin' then? I guess I got a right to go, if he does."

It was for Alfredo to answer that. "Who speaks of rights? I, too, have my scores. I was there when it began, so now I finish it. But you have fields to care for, and hay to seed."

"Ain't you got that, too? From your talk, the Rio Arriba's a regular garden of haying and seeding and such."

Alfredo laughed. "It all depends on the occasion. This time it is not. This time it is very barren ground. It makes little difference whether I am there or some place else."

"Huh," Pike said. "It's like I said—you was a barefaced liar before. An' still are, no doubt. I knowed it all along."

Pike ranged his eyes between them for a moment, sullen, like a man who knows that reasons are being invented for him to do a certain thing, and is unhappy, no matter that it fits his inclinations. Then, as if he couldn't help himself, his head turned on his shoulders, and his face filled up with longing as he looked westward through the pass.

"Go on, Pike," Alec said, quiet and gentle. "It's what you ought to have. You done all that anyone can ask of you, an' more. It ain't right that you take on something that don't really concern you. You got work of your own cut out for you yonder."

As if the work Alec spoke of put up a call that could be heard, Pike raised up in his stirrups, looking out. Then he sat again. He ran his fingers through the mane of his horse, watching the long strands separate.

"Was I to do as you say, would you be like to think me cowardly?"

"Lord God, no!" Alec said. "You know better'n that."

Pike looked up, the scowl beginning to edge away.

"You wouldn't think no worse of me?"

" 'Course not! How could I when it's me that's pushin' you? Go on, now, git. We'll see you soon enough. It ain't as if we're never going to meet again."

Pike began to smile a little now. "Come by my place, will you?"

"Hell, yes, you know it. Won't be but a couple of days, at most. Likely, we'll be riding on your tail."

Overhead, a hawk took out of a tree, sailed out over the pass upon the updraughts, swung in a wide and sweeping arc and slanted west. Like he felt the pull of it upon him, Pike trailed it with his eyes.

"Go on, now," Alec said. "Go chase that bird."

"Well—" Pike said, still trailing the wheeling hawk, still torn by indecision, but giving some now to the yondering in him.

"Git along, git along," Alec said, half singing it.

"If it's all right." Pike still watched. "If you won't hold it none against me."

"You know well enough by now it's all right. You hardly favor me to talk that way. I'm tired of hearin' of it. Get, now—move it."

The hawk was now far against the blue of deep hills. Pike turned again. His smile this time was full and broad, like that of a man who has fought a thing clean through and come out of it the way he felt he should.

"All right," he said. "All right—I'll do it the way you want me to."

It went quickly after that, now the doubts had been removed. Pike swung his horse back to the grade and looked around and waved.

"So long," he said. "I'll be lookin' for you."

They both waved, Alec and Alfredo.

"We'll be by," Alec said. "Keep your eye peeled."

"I'll be lookin' for you. Good luck. Does it look bad for you down there, pull out."

They waved again when Pike was too far to call to any more. There was a screen of brush, and they saw him one more time when he came out of that, but soon the trees below came up around him and he went out of sight.

Still they sat their horses for another minute, looking down, as if they had the chance yet for another sight of him.

"Well, we might as well push along," Alec said when Pike had gone for sure. He let his glance shift over to Alfredo, feeling partly friendly toward the man for having stayed, and partly angry at himself for having let him. "I don't know why you hung on."

Alfredo smiled. "It will make a story for my *nietos,* friend."

"You run a risk of not having any," Alec said. "You ever think of that?"

"So?" Alfredo shrugged. "All things in their time. But you are right. We run a risk. Have you thought of what those Indians will do if we are caught by them? Ho!"

"Uh-huh," Alec said. "There's law, too, don't forget. Stone's all the way outside it, now. There's nothing of the feud in what he's scheming to do down there. And does the law somehow show up and catch us, we'll swing as high as he."

"Yes," Alfredo said. "Death is very close to us—perhaps we had better live a while. Are you hungry?"

They were moving now. Alec glanced over at him again, and this time he grinned. "I suppose we ought to shoot that deer, at that. That's why we took out this morning, ain't it?"

CHAPTER ELEVEN

AFTER an hour they shot a deer, surprising it out of a covert where it had been nooning. A buck, not too thin from winter's wear, and already fattened some on spring browse. Cleaning it where it fell, they roasted up enough to satisfy their hunger of the moment, then wrapped some in dried grass to pack along in their saddle bags. What remained they left to hawks and coyotes and vultures.

Having eaten, they turned east, keeping above the pass and the Carrizozo Road, and holding it on the left. To the right some miles lay the borders of the Mescalero. Lincoln and San Patricio were a number of hours away and to be avoided. They were timing their pace by the sun, to reach Anders' place with the fall of darkness.

Riding through the afternoon, they spoke little. Alec was again plagued by his thoughts, his many doubts and questions.

A couple of times, glancing at Alfredo, he thought to throw up this last venture. But Alfredo had a right to be along—and he was old enough to make his choices and he had been with Tunstall in the old days. Too, he had been in the country long enough to have it known around that he had ridden with Stone, so that Stone's new outlawry could spill over on him as well.

At times he fretted about the contagion of Stone's madness, and worried about the madness in himself that was pulling him back to this last meeting with the man—yet this very craziness kept him moving to this rendezvous. He knew there would be no freedom for him anywhere so long as Stone was still living.

"*Caray*, the dark!" Alfredo said. "When have I seen it dark like this?"

"You got me," Alec said, hearing him clear enough, but having to stare to see him, though he rode not a dozen yards behind. "A good night for whatever happens, I'd say."

"Like the belly of a bear, *amigo*, far in his cave, and deep in winter sleep."

They were coming though a piece of hill land bordering on a valley that let down from higher country. The valley was a winding one and the water passing through it was an arm of Bonito, the creek which went through Lincoln town. Along the bottom of this valley, ringed around by hills, lay Anders' old range, and while they hadn't come in sight of the ranch, the ground and the shape of the hills they traveled said they were getting close to it.

After all these years of riding it they knew the country well enough to know their whereabouts, no matter the darkness of the night.

Off to the right now as they moved along, the shape of the hill they guided on was slowly breaking down.

"Can't be too far now," Alec said across his shoulder.

"No, I see the hill," Alfredo said. "The other one is out there somewhere, and the cut between them."

They rode on, watching the nearby hill grade off. Soon, beyond the loot of it, a black mass shaped up, so dim, though, and made so much of night and shadow that it seemed almost to be a thing imagined.

Still, Alec knew it to be there, for in between was a dark void, an emptiness, that gave out toward the far valley.

"I guess that's it, all right," he said when he was sure. "Black enough to be it, anyway."

Alfredo drew up beside Alec, who had stopped. "Yes, that would be it," he said, leaning forward, staring into the wall of night. "Do you see the buildings? *Caray,* how black!"

"Not yet, I don't. They're out there somewhere, though. We'll have to just keep headin' in until they show, that's all."

"So. We go. Do you want to ride, still? Or walk?"

Alec thought a second or two on that, holding his answer. As far as sound went, there wasn't too much difference. Afoot, though, they wouldn't be skylined, though the chance of their being seen was slim.

"Walkin' is best, I guess," he said. "Just as good to lead 'em in from here."

He started getting down, pulling his rifle from the scabbard at the saddle. "Best to lock your rowels, too," he said, reminded by the jingle of his own.

They walked from that point, and in five minutes had come to a point where a part of the swale turned into a draw. The draw went turning and snaking over the valley toward the south until it opened into the creek, where, in certain seasons, it carried run-off water from the hills. While Alec felt more than saw it, his memory told him what he knew of the draw, and he related other features of the valley to the place where they had entered it.

"Do we go through here," he said, "we can come up behind the buildings."

"Ho, I remember—yes. Well, the cover is good. But, will we be too close?"

"For clearin' out, you mean?"

"Well, that is something to think about. It could become a trap, perhaps. What of the sides of this draw? I forgot their height."

"As I remember, some high, some low. Do we need one, we can find a spot for breakin' out. There's still the ends, too—they're open. It's the cover I was thinkin' of."

"Yes, the cover will be worth the risk," Alfredo said.

They went on, leading their horses. The draw deepened. Other, smaller branches cut into it from one side or the other, and here and there the banks broke down allowing a feeling of openness. But mostly the walls loomed high on either side, giving them the cover they wanted, but making it needful to climb the slope from time to time to check their bearings.

After some minutes of this going, Alec could make out a mass of darkness blacker than the night, heavy and solid, and knew they had reached the trees surrounding the ranch buildings. Once he thought he saw the glimmer of a light, but though he stared until his eyes ached he lost it in the thick growth.

Finally they were at a part of the draw where the trees seemed to stand right over them. Alec could make out the yellow glowing of an oil lamp, too—nothing to give the outline of the buildings, but enough to judge the distance by.

"Maybe fifty yards," he told Alfredo. "I don't know as we can get much nearer."

"Who wants to get any nearer, friend?" Alfredo said. He laughed. "This is fine. What of the horses? Do we keep them here?"

"Might be better to move 'em off a ways. I don't like them bein' so close when something happens, if it does."

"All right," Alfredo said. "There is a place we passed back there where I can take them—the bank is low on both sides. Very good for getting out."

Alfredo went away, and Alec checked his rifle. He made sure he had a load in the breech, and then he took out his revolver and checked that, too. By then Alfredo had come back.

They lay on the bank of the draw while their eyes got used to the shapes of the buildings in the trees. Alec could see the light well, now, and it disturbed him. It was the first he'd thought of anybody being at the place, and he was bothered by it.

"Who do you think is in there?" Alfredo said after a time.

"In the cabin?" Alec said. "Some of Anders' boys, I'd say. I doubt there's been time enough to change crews yet, if they're going to change 'em. Likely, Harry Brittain's ramrod still. Wouldn't surprise me none if he was dealing a stud hand in there now."

"Do you think so? That's a good joke. One time he shot a horse from under me. Now we come to save his life."

Alfredo laughed, but with an irony that made Alec look at him.

"We ain't here to save no life of Harry Brittain," Alec said.

Still, it was a kind of joke, at that, being here, unknown to Harry Brittain, whom they'd fought, in order to bring an end to Stone, the one they'd ridden with so long.

But more than any joke, it was the crazy kind of thing that could happen to you in a range war; and beyond that, still, it was that special kind of craziness that overtook you when you'd run with Stone enough, or the likes of Stone.

For a second the ripeness of the thought brought up the familiar choke of anger to his throat, and in the next a feeling of despair rode over him—and there grew in him the wonder as to whether there would ever again be a time of freedom for him from this madness.

Not half a day ago he could have ridden off with Pike, and yet he hadn't. Over on the Rio Grande there would be all the things he'd wanted for so long; and still he'd passed them up in order to finish this. No matter he'd said to Pike this was the last fight, and that he and Alfredo would be along, the simple fact of his having come here seemed to say that the arrogant madness was in him, too, and that he was caught in it forever, for his whole life.

After a half-hour was gone, or a little more, Alec was beginning to wonder if Stone had been as serious as he'd seemed. Shifting his weight again upon the knotty ground, he took a look about them, searching out as far as he could see or hear. Nothing but the blackness answered him—that and silence.

Maybe Stone wasn't going to come, the thought grew in him. Could be the raid was just another of those dreams that Stone so often had, that nothing came of save a lot of blow. Still, them Indians gave this one a touch that didn't belong in a dream. And what of Harry Brittain? Ought he try to warn Harry in some way? But how could that be done without Brittain and his men filling himself and Alfredo with their bullets?

When he turned again he saw the star. Alfredo saw it, too, and pointed at it coming from the darkness in the west, rising into the curve of the sky.

"*Caray!*" he said. He crossed himself. "See it, Alec! A shooting star!"

They watched as it rose higher in its trail of light; at the top of its arc it turned and tipped away in a downward rush, fire streaking. When it fell behind the trees a ball of flame puffed out of the roof of one of the buildings, and Alec knew it was no shooting star. As he looked, a second flare came out of the west.

"Arrows," he said and, lying flat, reached to pull Alfredo down beside him.

"*Madre Dios,* so they come at last!" Alfredo said.

They had come, all right. There was no need of warning Harry Brittain any more. Everything seemed to happen all at once. Scrooching around behind a stand of grass, Alec could look through and see the buildings clearly now. In seconds, it seemed, the whole roof of one had caught ablaze. Stone had been right in judging that the dryness of the spring would let them burn, and every second seemed to drop more flaming arrows among them.

There was sound, too, by now, to go with the attack. The sound of Indian yelling put a crawling in Alec's flesh. It was as if a childhood time had come alive for him again—it might have been his family's place out there laced in flame, and the yelling the howling of Comanches. In a casement there appeared a man who was probably Harry Brittain. But for all the young remembrances that crowded in on Alec, it might have been his father, too, seeking a target for his rifle, and falling inward as a flaming arrow took him in the chest and set his clothes afire.

Off to the left, there was motion. As another building caught and flared, the circle of light spread out and grew, reaching farther and farther into the night, until far off in the shadows there were other, moving shadows. Some of these swept along swiftly, and would be mounted riders; others seemed a part of the shadows cast by brush or earth, and would be men who crept and crawled. There was the growing sound of rifle and carbine fire, and some chatter of six-guns.

Now that the surprise was over, there was shooting from the buildings, too. Alec could make out the spurts of gunfire, and now and then the figures of those defending. It was hard to tell how many were at the ranch, but from the firing he estimated less than half a dozen, likely. In daylight, when they could have used the range of their rifles, they might have held out; but in the deep of night against those fire arrows, and with the roof a lake of flame above them, their defeat was only a matter of time.

All this was something Stone had likely counted on, it came to Alec. It was almost as if he had an inner view of Stone's mind, the way it worked and looked at this. The moving shadows he had seen before were now quiet. Maybe Stone had been surprised to find the place defended, but now he knew, he wasn't satisfied to burn it only—now he had these Indians in his hands, it was plain he meant to hold them there, not riding off, until the ranch crew was forced to break and run for cover.

Of a sudden, Alec stood up. The glare of light was all around him, but he hardly noticed it. He felt a sickness in him, made of this, partly at what he saw, partly at that memory of another burning massacre which this had freshened.

"Alec! Alec! Man, get down!"

Alec scarcely heard Alfredo shouting. He felt himself surprised to see him, so taken was he with his wild anger.

"Get down!" Alfredo shouted. *"Madre Dios,* man, you stand in full view! What are you thinking, anyhow?"

"I'm going for Stone. I'm goin' to look for Stone."

"Stone?" Alfredo laughed. "Where will you find him in this? He's out there, hiding somewhere! Crazy man, get down, get down."

Alfredo tried to grab him, but Alec moved beyond his reach, and dropped into a crouch, ready to run for the trees.

"I'm goin'," he said across his shoulder. "Cover me as best you can. You'd better wait here."

Alfredo gave another shout, but only a part of it reached Alec. He was moving now. Ahead of him the trees stood black against the flaming buildings. Reaching out from them in his direction were dancing shadows.

He ran, and dropped, and ran again, watchful of the gun-fire coming from the shadows and the buildings. Here and there he found a bush or a rock to flop behind, but mostly his only cover was grass. It was hard to tell if he had been seen and fired at, but there was lead enough flying around him. Once he heard Alfredo's rifle boom, and far off on the left he saw an Indian stumble from the shadows, light up with reflection from the buildings' glare, and spill over.

When he looked again the shadows were beginning to fall about him, and then he was among the trees, leaning against one, breathing hard and feeling the sweat drain down his flanks. On either side of the trunk the earth was bright as day. He felt the nearness of the scorching heat and heard the rumble of the flames and the men in the buildings shouting to each other.

He humped from tree to tree, working toward the far side of the buildings, around to where he had first seen the arrow streaks. As the attack had come from that direction, it was likely Stone was there, directing operations.

He had only covered half the distance when it seemed as if the sun itself had come alive in the night. A spout of flame ripped out of the building where the men were fighting. Parts of the blazing roof rose into the air on the roaring updraft. Flaming wreckage swung high above the trees and fell like torches all about him on the ground. Heavy beams and timbers crashed down upon screaming men. In the second that the roof gave way, there was no night, but only a brilliant noon, and a massive thunder shook the earth beneath him.

Then there was another screaming, that of Indians. All this time they had waited, now they came. Hugging the ground against the brilliance, Alec saw them coming from the shreds of shadow in the west and south. There were perhaps a dozen of them, heading toward him in their white clouts, some afoot and some mounted, like screeching devils.

He looked for Stone and Clint and Roy, but in the pell-mell charge it was impossible to search out individuals. The defenders were coming out of the blazing building now, those who still lived. Some were injured or smoke-poisoned and stumbled blindly in all directions. Most ran through the doorway, but a few spilled through the flaming windows, black and smoking. One or two of them, who had kept their wits and weapons, knelt for aim in order to meet the Indians, but most just ran as if the world was at an end.

He was caught in the mixup before he could work back to cover. A man ran by him with a shriek, his clothing blazing, raw meat stripping redly from his back. Another took off for the Indians, running blind and wobbly-legged, until an arrow bore him to the ground, where he lay jerking. Off to one side Alec caught a motion, and just in time swung his rifle at a mounted Indian. The fire was on his face, and the yell was halfway out of him when Alec's heavy bullet tore him from his saddle—he raised a plume of dust that came up golden in the light. Bucking and kicking, the horse shied so that it slammed against another. The rider cartwheeled in the air and spilled beneath the pounding hooves.

The melee got too wild to follow after that. The Indians and the stumbling, fighting men were all around him. Some were even in the trees behind him now; from them came yells, shouts and gunfire.

There came a new sound—at first it was a part of the others but as it neared it grew distinct. From the south and west came a blur of movement into the light, and Alec made out the sameness of the horses and riders. The men wore blue with yellow stripes along their trouser legs, and their equipment shone and sparkled in the firelight.

He wasn't surprised to see the soldiers—nothing in all the years of outrage in this land had come up to this for violence and, if anything, he wondered that they hadn't shown up earlier. Still, the Mescalero was a distance away from Fort Stanton and likely the Agent hadn't known the meaning of the gathering at camp in time to send the word.

He was running now. Over his shoulder he could see the troopers in a file, heading toward the buildings. They were nearing quickly now and he began to feel his senselessness in having come here at all. He ran, marveling that he'd thought that he could ever stop these savages, once Stone had primed them. He ran, knowing there was a chance he would be trapped, wishing he had gone with Pike, as he had planned.

Then he just ran. He stopped his mind to Stone and all regrets involved. The trees blocked the troopers from his view. Off to his right, the buildings flared and burned, and he went by them, humping for the darkness beyond.

About him were burning fragments of roof, boards and shingles thrown up by the updraft and carried away on the heated air. Once he stumbled over a writhing, smoking body, whether Indian or white, he could not tell. Another time he ran full tilt against an Indian and knocked him spinning. His third encounter came when he was past the trees and looking for the draw and Alfredo, and an Indian was there.

Alec didn't see him right away—the Indian came out of the earth before him. It was as if he had been waiting there for some-one, and with the light on him, Alec knew it was the renegade. The redskin poised a knife and leaped forward, running.

Oddly, it seemed to Alec that he had a certain leisure to study out the details of the familiar face, the streaming clout, the dirty headband and the glinting knife the renegade carried. The Indian wore moccasins whose toes were pointed, and there was no emotion in his face at all—his face was blank.

Alec swung his rifle from the hip, but knew it would not come around in time. When he squeezed the trigger, he could feel the recoil at the time of impact with the Indian. The gun roared off to the left; the blow of the buck was from the right, and the weapon flew out of his grasp. Thrown off balance, he and the renegade danced and tilted in a quarter circle before they fell.

They landed rolling, locked together for a second, then loos-ened by the jar. Alec saw the knife go up and whicker down. He felt a burning on his side. It filled him with a fear and strength, and he fought.

They were locked together for the moment, rolling, surging, one against the other, while the breath tore in and out of them. He could hear the renegade panting at his ear, his breath rasp-ing as Clint's had that other time. Alec could smell him, too, the unwashed stink of him, the grease, the sweat. He felt the slip-periness of the other, and the warmth and wetness along his own side. The knife was down there somewhere, too, along that side, gripped in the hand he locked beneath his arms.

It was coming free, though, the knife was. No matter what force he put into his arms, the knife was working loose. Down there along his burning side, the sweat and salty blood were oil-ing his grip so that it soon must break.

All at once he saw the knife in the air above him. It went up so fast he seemed to see it before knowing it was loose. Up it went, and the Indian rose with it; his eyes were looking straight down, and they were flat in his head like those of a snake about to strike.

Then, past the Indian's head he saw his boot, and it surprised him that it should be there. On the heel of it he saw the spur, the fire on the pointed rowels threw off a gleam and a flash. He had no memory of lifting it, but as the renegade rose for his downward lunge he hooked the leg and rolled.

He threw his whole weight into the roll and the spur sank into the side of the renegade's neck, the rowels locked, the long spikes sharp and pointed. He heard the choking shriek, saw the chest above him arching back and over. The knife sailed high in the air, and blood shot dark and shining over the chest and clout. Through his leg, he felt the jerking spasms of the renegade as he drove the spur in harder ....

Alec was some minutes getting his spur from the torn throat. It was nothing he thought of, though. He thought of nothing at all as he worked it loose, saw the drench of blood upon him, and rolled over on his stomach. Pushing up, he stood on both feet, swaying. Beyond the renegade he saw his rifle. He stooped to pick it up, rose again and went ahead.

He came to the draw and, hunching down, tried to sit and slide to the bottom, but he went wrong some way and lost his balance. He fell, slid and rolled, threw up stones and earth until the bottom stopped him. His rifle slammed across his chest.

He got up slowly. His side burned now like a faggot had been in it. He put his hand to it, but the feel of bare ribs against his fingers scared him and he took his hand away. Now he saw Alfredo coming toward him with the horses. Alfredo stopped, made sure of him, and then came on.

"Mother of God!" Alfredo said. "What have you done?" He touched the bloody shirt. "Have they killed you? Alec! Look at you!"

"It ain't all mine," Alec said. "The blood, that is. Some of it came out of the renegade."

"Holy Mary! Enough is yours! Where are you hurt?"

"It's all right," Alec said. "In the ribs, is all. Most is from the renegade."

His horse was there, and Alec leaned on it. All at once his legs were very wobbly under him. He tried to get his foot up into a stirrup, but couldn't make it. His rifle fell. Alfredo ran around behind to push him up. He kept talking all the while.

"Where have you been? Holy Mother of Jesus! What a sight you are. Still, you walk. That Indian—may he roast in hell! Is it deep in the ribs? We must leave this place!"

He went on that way, pushing, heaving. Alec had the pommel in his hands—as he pulled, exquisite sheets of pain flared up and down his side. Finally, he lay panting over the pommel, feeling sticky with sweat and blood.

After that there was a time when things were not so clear. He became aware of motion, and knew that they were going down the draw. Sounds came and went within his consciousness—sometimes he could hear Alfredo talking, at other times he heard the roaring of the fires; still, again, it was the yelling of the Indians or the troopers or the ragged bursts of gunfire. Once a horse went down the edge of the draw above them, pounding hard.

By the time he could sort things out again the draw was lifting and they came out of it into the cut that passed between the low hills. As they were in the open now, Alfredo yelled for him to hurry.

Still, he stopped once to look across the level valley. The blaze stood high in the trees and the buildings were sinking into the redness of the earth. Against the light he saw the silhouettes of Indians and troopers; sometimes there were those who might be what remained of the defenders.

Perhaps some of the shapes he saw were Stone and Roy and Clint. It seemed a long time ago since he had thought of them, and now he wondered what had happened to them. It was hard to see how they could live through this, and he was ready to believe they hadn't, even though he had no way of being sure. Then he was too tired to wonder any more. He had come to do what he could do, and had failed. But it had been madness in the first place. His and Stone's.

He let it go, giving up for the moment. Ahead, the hills swelled large to either side and soon, when he looked back again, the light was gone.

CHAPTER TWELVE

THAT night they traveled through the mountains toward the pass along the Carrizozo Road. A part of the time they held the road itself; some of the time they rode among the trees and brush upon the unmarked hills or in the valleys. The times they took to the brush and trees were when they thought they might be trailed, either by the Army, a posse, or Stone's renegades. Aside from an awareness of the changing ground, Alec took small notice of their surroundings. It was now Alfredo's business how they went, or where, and such awareness as he had was limited to periods of clearness which came and went according to their own fashion. Once when they worked along a steep grade, he awoke in mid-air, spilling from his seat, and he remembered that. Another time, when the line between unconsciousness and wakefulness became too fine to know, he rammed his side against the pommel of his saddle. And that stayed with him, too; the remembrance of the pain, like a red mark in an even weave of gray or black.

It went that way through days and nights of travel through the mountains. Mostly, constant weariness claimed him, and so made him unresponsive to what happened. Still, he had a knowledge of their need to get away, of the feel of cold as the land's height increased, of the scent of familiar pine, of halts to see if they were folllowed, of long by-passes going around a ranch or village, of rests and mealtimes.

After a while they were in the desert of the Tularosa basin. Little burrowing owls sat under pallid growths of bayonet and watched them pass with blank eyes. Kangaroo rats held their panting bodies to the shade of nests against the brilliant heat. Now and then a snake put up its head from out its coil of sand and menaced them, while its tongue went out in a questioning flicker. It was a place of malapai and ashes and sand, of light so glittering that the eyes were pained to squint; Alec felt the skin stretched across his skull shrivel on the bone. Overhead, the sun set up a pounding in him like a copper gong.

They were four days going over this. Still fearful of pursuit, they left the road entirely and held to trails wild animals had made. Trails so thin and finely marked they might have been imagined except they followed a natural contour in their wanderings. Often there were no trails. And often trails existed only in Alfredo's memory; remembrances of old trails related to him by the elders of his family who had made the long *jornadas* up the Rio Grande from Mexico. Trails, if they were trails at all, which led across the lava barrens, black and livid in the shaking air. Those which, unmarked, went over gypsum fields so white that even the thought of them was blinding. There were places where not even lizards thrived; there were other places so spare of any kind of life that the sand and stone ran on unbroken and unrelieved until it beached against the blue and shimmering mountains.

There was water, though. Drawing on his knowledge of the "old ways," Alfredo once found it deep beneath a shattered mesquite tree. Another time, ancient Indian writings on a wall of rock revealed a small and natural tank into which a deep earth spring seeped drip by slow drip. Still again, upon the end of a panting and waterless afternoon, they stumbled on a ragged-spined *bisnaga*—opened with their knives, its storage cup held enough moisture to see them through the following day.

The days came, passed across the burning sky and simmered into the flaming dusk at evening. In Alec's mind they poured through one another and away like molten metal, the heat rising to its scorching noons and afternoons and then diminishing as dark came on the land, but never leaving quite. The mildest effort of the body became a heroic thing. To keep a lucid thought for any length of time became an undertaking. The aching hours in the saddle made his injured side a goad to him—all his bones and joints went stiff from riding in a certain way so as to favor it. Getting down to rest a while would make him sick with pain; sometimes it was better just to sit and take it until they started on again.

He tried to dress the gash as best he could, but as he had no proper bandaging or anything, it was often better to leave it be. Were it only for the pain and stiffness, the natural way of healing would be best, perhaps, but there was a part of the wound that worried him and kept him fussing at it—the part in the soft flesh below the raking skid along the ribs. Upon the ribs themselves, there came to be a crust, firm and hard, but underneath, such scab as formed kept sloughing off, so that an ooze came out. When the ooze was red, the only thing that bothered him was pain, but when the ooze turned yellowish there grew a fright in him to fool with it, and even to look at it.

After a while he took a fever, too, a thing he knew to be related to the wound. It came and went in waves of heat and cold, so that sometimes he'd be halfway frozen at noon, and in the middle of the night he might be sweating bullets. Peculiar things began to happen to his eyes and vision, and in a while he found he couldn't trust them any more.

It was at a time when he was cold and dizzy both that they came up a rise, and when they stopped, the downward slope gave off to water in the distance, blue and full of shimmer in the bright sunlight. He didn't believe Alfredo when the Mexican said it was the Rio Grande—he knew enough about mirages, and he knew about the ways the fever tricked him, too. Still, the image stayed with him this time, when they descended to it; stayed and shimmered brown and blue, depending on the light and shallows. And when he felt it slosh against his boots and legs he was convinced.

CHAPTER THIRTEEN

I T WAS funny how a river put a man in mind of humankind, Alec often thought. This one now, the Rio Grande, was like an old man, coming from nobody could say where, flowing on past Pike's place and away on off to yet another place that nobody could be sure of, far off to the sea. Slow, it went, and pokey, mostly, spreading itself to the sun, taking its ease in its sandy bed, lolling an hour away in a quiet pool, and going on. From far off in the north it rustled down through soaring timber, into slots of black granite. Here, in this sun-baked middle country it grew quiet, thoughtful, passing under cliffs where the *antiguas* had built houses in an ancient time, crossing old trails where the Spanish had gone marching in their gilded armor; slipping below the ruins of pueblos, weathered and worn by wind and heat and rain so that they sought to join the mother earth again. Going on through yellowed canyons, under thirsty banks of greening cottonwoods, through plains of black volcanic cinders, through the shaking sunlight, the blue and shimmering haze, and on and on.

During the week he spent with Pike, Alec had the time to watch the river, to note its dreaming ways and to wonder at the things it might have seen and known of. At first they had him on a bed of old smooth pine laced under with rawhide, lying on a straw tick. The bed was in a room with yeso-plastered walls, low and white. The floor was plain adobe, made hard as stone with ox blood, and overhead, the vigas were of pine, dark with age. Over in one corner stood an old trastero, where his clothes were kept. On top of it stood a wooden *bulto* of St. Francis, carved and painted in the Spanish way with dark brows and a pointed beard. On the dobe floor was a rug, red and black and gray—a Navaho, from what he knew about them.

There was a window, too, in a wall a yard thick, which gave out over the meadows toward the clouds of trees along the water. Hunching up a certain way in bed, he could look out and see the cattle on the *vegas,* and the silver threads of ditches running from the headgate of the main *acequia* through the fields. Sometimes there were men among the cattle, or in the hay fields farther down by the water. Across the river he could see the terraced walls of a pueblo, all of earth, and spreading out in steps and levels. Sometimes there were Indians working in the garden plots around it; often there were others wrapped in sheets against the sun, leaning on the walls the livelong day, just looking out, as if expecting something. At night the sound of drums and chants came over the river as they made their ceremonials to the gods for good fortune with their crops.

From all that Pike had said in times they'd spoken of it, Alec came to find it a familiar place. Things he saw were those he'd known of in advance, and had expected—the look of the river flowing on, the fields of hay and other crops, the ditches. This was a rich and growing land.

Yet there was a thing here he hadn't known of, that he'd had no way of knowing, an ironic situation. Pike told him of it, laughing and joking, himself surprised. It related to the old man who'd cared for things while he was gone. It now developed he was uncle to the girl who'd ridden on the stage—the plain girl, the one that Alec had talked to in Lorenzo's. Her name was Ruth Hagan.

It was the second day he recognized her. All he knew the first time she came was that he was bedded in a strange and quiet place, and that a woman came to do for him. Partly blank with fever still, he hardly cared who fooled with him—for all he knew, she might have been some squaw from across the river, or some neighboring native woman brought in to help out.

All he remembered of that first time were sensations—the warmth of water on his skin, the sharp carbolic smell, the feel of fire when the gash was cleaned, and at last the pressure of a binding on it. Then she went away. She said nothing at all to him while she was in the room, that he remembered, and save for the binding and the odor that stayed on, he might have dreamed her.

The second time was different, though. That time he was awake and clear of fever. When she came, he turned his head and saw her set the basin on the wooden table. With it there was soap, a bottle of carbolic, and a number of folded clothes. When she turned, she caught his glance.

"Well," she said, "you're awake this time."

He smiled and nodded at her. "I'm awake, all right," he said. "I guess you came before. I remember someone—don't remember who, though."

"Yes, I came before, yesterday afternoon. That's when they brought you in."

For a moment she was busy at the table, and there was nothing for him to do but look at her. He watched her choose a cloth and put it into the water in the basin. In the clear light of the room her eyes and wheat-straw hair were as he'd carried them in his memory of Lorenzo's, and of the stage, too. Her dress was different, though—she now wore a colored skirt and white blouse. With her eyes away from him, he was able to study her unobserved, and see all he'd seen in her those other times.

When the cloth was soaking well, she knelt beside the bed to take off the binding. The light shone through her hair and lay along the contours of her neck and shoulders, putting a softness on them.

"I know who you are," he said. "I saw you once—twice, as a matter of fact."

He smiled, feeling the pleasure of this place, and of this meeting with her. But she ignored the smile.

"I know who you are, too," she said. "Pike told me some about you. But I remember seeing you." She watched her fingers working at the knot that held the binding. "And I know what you are."

Her eyes were down, but Alec was able to sense the resistance in her—a resentment.

"What d'you mean by that?" he said.

"You know what I mean," she said. "You were there—I was there. I don't see the need to talk about it."

"Why not?" he asked. "If you were there, you saw what happened. I've got nothing to hide."

"Aren't you hiding now?" she said, still looking down. "If not, why aren't you over in that country facing it? Why don't you go to the law and tell what happened?"

"You don't know about that place," he said. "I'd as leave go into a thicket of bears, unarmed. In feudin', the law rides with the strongest."

"You told me once it was a beautiful place," she said. "I remember that. Well, in fact. In Mr. Morales' place, in Lincoln."

"So, and once it was," he said. "I said this was, too, if you remember. I was thinkin' more of this place then. There's nothing wrong here."

She shrugged, the light shifting upon her shoulders as she moved. Her glance passed over him, holding for a second and then going on.

"I can't say I've seen much difference yet. So far, both places are the same to me. Even the people are the same." At last the knot came free, and she began to lift the binding off. "Maybe it's the people make it that way."

Alec laughed, although he hardly felt like it. Quarreling didn't belong among the thoughts he had had about this girl, and yet some kind of devil drove him on. It seemed, almost, as if it was the only way they had to come to know each other, that argument went more to the depths of a person than gentle talk. On his part, his touchiness might partly be caused by the feeling that he didn't have much time before he'd have to run again.

"Yes, we're sure some bunch," he said. "We'd sooner kill a man than eat. You get that way in a while."

"From what I've seen, I can believe it," the girl said, her mouth a firm line, her fingers swift at her work.

He laughed again, feeling a certain pleasure in the look of vinegar in her face, no matter he knew the wrong of speaking as he did.

"You ought to see us when we're really going. Take Alfredo, if you like. Alfredo makes a special thing of bashing heads."

"Maybe it's the company he keeps," she said. "Maybe he can't help himself. He's got the look of a villain, though."

"And then take Pike," he said. "Pike likes slitting throats. He's got an ear for the sound of air whistling in and out."

"I expect that could be true," Ruth Hagan said. "No doubt, though, he's rather young to know his own mind yet. Mostly, the young just follow."

"That kind of puts the taint on me, it looks like," Alec said.

"You're their leader, aren't you? That's what Pike said, anyway. You ought to know—he said you had the answers."

The girl worked, her eyes down, the color rising in her cheeks. For the first time now he saw the length of her lashes and the way her neck curved down below her ear. Her ears were small and delicate and drew a special notice from him.

He was angry now, partly at himself, and tried to rise up on his elbows, but a part of the binding gripped the scab and sent a stab of fire through him. Panting, he lay back again while sweat poured over him.

"I'm sorry if it hurts," she said, her eyes still fixed on what she was doing.

"I don't see why you should be," Alec said, clamping his teeth against the agony. "It's nothing to you. No doubt, you feel a hurt to me is fitting."

"I didn't say that," she said. "You're putting words in my mouth."

"You just ain't got around to saying it, is all. Keeping it in is all the same as speakin' out, given the thought is there."

"I don't see how you can tell my thoughts," she said, getting the binding free at last, and dropping it on the floor. She turned, her face a high color, and took the wet cloth from the basin.

"You don't? I can tell, all right. You're thinkin' there's a lot you'd rather do than this right now. Likely, you feel dirtied, just to touch me."

They were strangers to each other, but they carried on like people who'd been married years. They'd only met, but for the feeling built between them of a sudden, they might be lovers finding fault with one another. It was strange and queer to Alec, this intensity of feeling—it was as if each of them felt the right and need to plumb the other, and now was angered at some lack.

"I don't feel one way or the other about it," she said, putting the fresh cloth against him now, but softly. "Somebody has to do it."

"You don't have to, though," he said, driven to goad her, still. "You don't have to care for me. I thought you was carin' for your uncle."

"Him," she said, and let it go, as if the one word might be all her uncle needed. "Keep your arm clear now. Higher, please. There. Hold it like that." She put the cloth aside, reaching back for the carbolic and a new dressing.

"Hardly anyone to your liking out here, is there?" Alec said. "Surprised you came at all."

"Sometimes, when you're lonely, you seek kin," she said, reaching the dressing ties around him now, bringing her breast against him, its soft curve pressing. Her glance touched his as she drew away again. "You can't help it any if kin are different than you thought. You learn, though, then you bide your time."

She was finished now. She stood up and gathered her things together, her face still flushed, partly from anger, partly, perhaps, from something else. He couldn't tell, except he had a sudden memory of a doe he had once startled in the timber.

Still it seemed he couldn't let her go without having the final word.

"If you don't like it here," he said, "why don't you leave? You're free enough to go, I guess. That's one thing out here, anyway—you're free to choose."

"Save for money, yes," she said. In the open door, she turned to look at him, the latch in her hand. "I guess you know what money means. I've seen you at your work."

PART III
FAST MAN—LAST MAN

CHAPTER FOURTEEN

OR all Alfredo had had to say about the heat of the days in the Rio Abajo, and of the sweat supposed to flow through the *acequias* at certain times, still the nights were cool enough in that country. After a few days, when Alec was up and around, they would often have a little fire in front of the casa in the evenings. Perhaps this was because they'd lived so long out of doors, perhaps because there was a fragrance to *piñon* smoke not given by a fireplace, perhaps it was just the pleasure of sprawling on a hide beneath the stars. Whatever it was, it was a natural thing to them.

They were pleasant evenings, there in the dooryard, with the fire warming them, the smell of the country in the woodsmoke, the taste of *piñon* nuts upon their tongues.

Often one of the field hands came with his guitar to play for them, and they would sing the old songs: *Cielito Lindo, La Comparsa, Andalucia, Malaguena, Adios Muchachos,* and others, the music soft and lilting as it told of olden times and places, and having the certain sadness that runs through Spanish music, thoughtful-like, and asking the meaning of a thing.

Sometimes they would just sit, the three of them, Pike, Alfredo and himself, cracking *piñones* in their teeth, and talking out on whatever might come to mind.

"What did I tell you, friend," Alfredo might start off, "here in the Rio Abajo the heat is such we must sit in the out of doors."

"It ain't so hot a fire doesn't feel good, though," Pike might answer. "An' I notice you're sittin' plenty close to it, Alfredo."

Then, as they had opened on that subject, Pike might turn to Alec and say, "Alec, you ought to give this place some thought. There's plenty of good land hereabouts for a man as cares to work it. You got only to look an' make your choice."

Alec would have to tell about the mountains, then. It was hard to figure out the spell they cast upon a person, and so made other land of no account beside them—still, he owed the effort to Pike on many counts.

"Well, we got the Sandias almost at your back," Pike might say when Alec had done the best he could. "They ain't but a couple of hours east."

"A couple of hours is pretty far off," Alec would explain. "I got to be in them."

That was how the mountain talk would always end; it was like they came to a cliff and there was no way down, and so they had to leave off there.

Then they would fork off on other things, the Rio Arriba, say, or whether or not the dancing of the Pueblos would bring rain, and if such rain as came would come before July. Everybody knew that rain before July would mean a wet and bountiful season. It was lazy talk, the talk of men who had the time to stick a straw between their teeth, feeling for a word as much for the sound it might make in the ear as for the meaning of it.

Sometimes they talked about the girl, who lived down the road a ways in a little hovel with her uncle. Though she never came to spend the evening with them at the fire, Alec now and then would catch himself glancing in that direction, as if his eyes played traitor to him in some way and sought for her without the leave of his mind. In some strange way he couldn't figure out, he felt peculiar when they talked of her.

Like the time Pike said to him, while they were lolling on the cowhides with their smokes, the fire going—laughing, he threw it out like bait.

"Alec, was I you, I might think twice before I went away and left a pretty girl like her, just on account of a yearning for a pile of mountains."

"I don't know what she might have to do with it," Alec said. "There's more to be thought of in a girl than being pretty. Prettiness wears thin."

"How come you know that?" Pike said, as if he was surprised that Alec might have thought of such a thing. "You talk like you been married fifty years."

"Or like he's had his thoughts on it some," Alfredo said.

Alec stretched and hunched around the cowhide, uneasy of a sudden.

"It just occurred to me, is all," he said. "A man don't have to be married himself to read the sign."

This made Alfredo chuckle to himself, and glance at Alec.

"What kind of sign is that?" Pike said, taken with this new thought. "She's pretty, ain't she? An' she's plenty good at doin' for you. I'll bet she knows her way around a stove. Moreover, she's free and on the country."

"Plenty feisty, too," Alec said, wishing they'd quit speaking of her.

"Feisty?" Pike said. "I hadn't noticed any feistiness. She hasn't shown any feistiness to me."

"As with a mare, it depends upon the stallion," Alfredo said, laughing again to himself, as if at a private joke.

"Say," Pike said. "I wonder if that's so. Now I think of it, she did say Alec looked a little dangerous." He slid a glance at Alec, grinning wide. "Maybe it's on account of he's been bad so long, ramming around the country like a bloody cutthroat, leading us all astray." He fetched a slap at Alec's leg. "Given you ain't interested, maybe I might court her some myself."

"You do that," Alec said, glad to put an end to it.

Then there were the times her uncle came to sit with them a spell. Squatting down beside them in his jeans and whiskers, he would talk about the old days, the days when he had fought with Kearney as a scout—those days that looked the better for the time that lay between them, when the land was young, when he was young, himself. Like he might have been a log cast up upon the river bank, the river leaving him to dry and rot, he made a great complaint about those vanished times, now gone without him.

"I tell 'e, lads, it's sp'iled," he'd say, and pound his bony fist upon the ground to drive the point, his beard stained brown and yellow with tobacco juice. "The whole of the country's gone to wrack. You take a land that gets plowed under and farmed over, and beat beneath a million feet, stock and people both—she won't last. You can't expect it to."

It seemed that Pike had heard this all before, because he would only laugh and say, "Hell, Jud, there's been people in this valley a thousand years, more'n a thousand years; them Pueblos're farmers. An' look at you—you took up land yourself an' tromped all over it."

"Sure, an' I regret it plenty, too. You notice, though, I didn't take up much. Just enough to raise a patch of beans. Not like one of them dons, who takes the whole of a country to himself."

Another time, like a man who measured his wealth in terms of what he didn't have, he said, "Land's a freight upon a person. The more he has, the less he's really got. He's free according to the little he can get along with. And not only land, either."

Still another time, he said, "People!" and gave a snort. "People, they're the ruin of a country. If only you could keep the people out. More'n once I said them very words to Kearney when I showed the way. First it's soldiers comin' in. Then they get the country safe and sure, an' farmers come. Then the farmers get a taste for boughten things, an' merchants come, diggin' in your pockets. Then, by hell, it's women, women comin' in alone—ain't that something, now, I ask you?"

That was one of the times he brought the jug. It seemed the jug was apt to make him feel more keenly the loss of all he'd come to in the past, and make him yearn to stir himself and follow the visions of the bygone westering.

With his jug between his knees, he sat upon his cowhide, gazing into yesterday with glassy eyes.

"I should have gone with 'em," he said, as if scarce a day or two had passed since he had given up his trails. The "them" meant all those others who'd gone on and left him in this place, stranded.

"It's all the same, no matter where you go these days," Pike said.

"The hell you say, boy. There's places still—don't be tellin' me what's out there." As if he had the power to see across the river in the dark, he stretched his scrawny neck beneath his matted whiskers and looked out. "There's places still—plenty of them. All they're needin' is the finding." He settled back again, and looked around. "By hell, I'd like to go and find 'em, damn it all. Wasn't for this niece of mine, I might."

He took a drink from the jug and, setting it down again, stared a long time at the throat of it.

"Damn it all, I'd like to, sure enough. Now that you're back, boy, I might yet."

Alec felt he learned things sitting by the fire on those evenings. He had a notion of the country filling up, of change. Perhaps the things the old man said about the land were true— maybe he was right. It was easy to see why he might feel as he did. And it was easy to see why Ruth, his niece, might speak of her uncle in the slighting way she did.

Then it was another night, the last night, as it happened. During the day, Alfredo had gone, but he was back in time to see the fire kindled in the dooryard. He came in dusty and grimy, and with a look of having ridden hard and long.

"Hey, *amigo*," he said to Alec when he'd washed himself and joined them at the burning *piñon* branches, "how do you go today? Do you hurt any more?"

"Hey, *amigo,* yourself," Alec said. "No, I don't hurt any more. Where you been?"

"Well, I was here and there. Not all of us can lie in a bed and have a lady stroke our brows." He hunkered down beside the fire and put a coal to his *cigarro.* "To tell you the very truth, I rode to Albuquerque."

Alec hunched around upon his cowhide. "Albuquerque? What was you doin' there?"

"Looking, friend, looking." He touched Alec with his hand and smiled. "Can you ride? Are you good enough to ride?"

Alec gave up lying down and sat up, easing his elbow under him to brace himself. "Sure," he said. "Sure, I'm good enough to ride. What did you see in Albuquerque, anyway, that makes you want to ride?"

"Well, I see *soldados* there."

"So? That ain't unnatural. They come up from Craig and other places. Likely, some are stationed there. It ain't surprising you should see some."

"Well, perhaps," Alfredo said. "But I saw the guidon from Fort Stanton in their hands, too. A little body of men was riding, and they flew it at their head. Very pretty."

"Was there many of them?" Alec said.

Alfredo shook his head. "No. Only a few. Just a little handful."

Alec said, "Could be they were doing courier duty?"

Alfredo nodded, blowing a puff of smoke above him.

"Yes, that could be," he said.

"Could be they weren't too," Alec said flatly.

He looked away across the fire into the dark that lay upon the river and the trees. Far away he heard the Indians chanting to their gods about the crops. For the first time it came to him how fine a sound that was, homey-like, and speaking of a settled permanence. Almost, he would like to be among them, chanting and dancing, too; free of flight, free of scouting out his backtrail. For the first time in a week the weight he had put aside came down again, full and heavy, seeming greater than ever, because of his having shed it for a while.

Drawing on his smoke, he found the taste gone sour, and he threw it into the fire.

"Yes, I'm good enough to ride," he said. "Morning suit you?"

He was dressed when she came in that time, dressed and sitting on the bed, his gear around him, ready to leave. There was no reason to think she might have changed, just because of his going. There was still that same remoteness in her gray eyes, that same resenting stiffness in the way she moved.

She came in, set the basin on the wooden table, and put her cloths to soaking. Then she came to him and took the binding off—this time it came easy, not clinging as it had before. Underneath, the scab was dry and firmly hard.

"I guess I ought to thank you for your trouble," Alec said, wanting to make his peace with her. "It was plenty bad before you took hold of it and fixed it."

"There's no need for thanks," **R**uth Hagan told him. "I'd have done the same for anyone."

Alec felt his ears becoming red. It was like she couldn't stand to have a good thing said to her, without having to turn it back upon the giver.

"Well, I'm sorry to put you out," he said. "No doubt, there're better things to do."

She shrugged, hardly giving a look at him.

"I don't know it makes much difference. A person's got to earn his keep somehow. And it's a thing I know a little of."

"Even so, you're likely glad it's over and done with," Alec said, still needled.

"You keep saying what I ought to think," she said. "Do you make a habit of putting words in people's mouths for them, thinking for them?"

"Only when I know what they want to say," he said.

"Maybe it's no worse than putting a gun on them, at that," she said.

After that, he sat quiet in his anger, watching her, seeing the sureness of her hands, the shaping of her shoulders to her slim neck. For all the plainness that he had marked in her, she was a person of uncommon shape and beauty, too—and it was a thing of puzzlement that one so endowed in spirit and body should carry in her such bitterness.

For a woman, he thought, it was bad to be unwanted.

She was finished with him now and he stood up. While she turned to sort her cloths and bindings out, he gathered his shirt about him again and buttoned it. The knowledge that it was the last time she would do for him had made him more aware of her than ever, and he put out his hand to touch her. She turned, seeming surprised that there was more to say.

"I meant it, thanking you," he said, and felt suddenly awkward. "I appreciate it, and I'm sorry to put you out."

"It's all right," she said.

"I suppose my bunch is what you say we are," he said. "I don't know that we're quite so bad, and maybe you'll come to see that, too, some day."

"That might be," she said, and then seemed surprised by the admission. Standing with her hands together at her waist, her fine gray eyes cast down, she seemed to have been suddenly stripped of her defenses and of her will to make a fight of every word and thought. She was as she had been when he had seen her for the first time, before their points of view had clashed.

It was then the impulse took him, born partly of sorrow for her loneliness, and partly of an inner hunger. He felt filled with urgent words, but before they had the chance to tumble out of him he reached out to her again. That time, instead of merely touching her, he took her by the arm and drew her to him. As he bent down to kiss her, she raised her face to look at him, and as if she couldn't help herself, her arms came up around his neck and he could feel her press against him, soft and warm, the scent of her a thing to make the blood pound in his head, her lips softly moist against his own.

How long he held her so, he could not tell. All he knew was that some crazy thing had happened, something he could scarcely believe. He held her tight against him, and the warmth and fragrance of her flooded over him.

Then he could feel her arms come free—she put her hands against his shoulders, pushing, and he let her go. As she drew back from him, her eyes still held him, wide and startled and unbelieving.

"Oh," she said, and as if he had sullied her some way, she drew her arm across her lips. "Oh," she said again, staring at him.

He tried to take her arm again, but she evaded him. Backing off against the wooden table, she put her hands to her face, as if she couldn't bear to look at him any longer, knowing what she'd done.

"Don't," she said. "Please. Don't. Go away—please—go away."

Watching her, he felt a dullness coming over him. She was telling him that what had happened was an error, a mistake, and that she hadn't meant it. It was as if a door he had had a glimpse through had been slammed before him. Suddenly the warmth he had felt for her turned chill in him and, reaching down, he gathered his gear together with a sweep of his arm.

"I'm goin'," he said, knowing that anger bristled in his voice, but not caring. "Don't worry none—I'm gittin' now. You don't have to hide no more."

"Yes, go," she said, her eyes like cold fire as she took her hands away. Her voice was higher as he reached the door. "And stay away," she said. "And stay away from Pike, too. You got him into enough."

"So, and I got him out of it, too," he said and, stepping out, felt the dobe dust spill down upon him from the corbel over the heavy door as he slammed it shut behind him.

CHAPTER FIFTEEN

RIDING north again along the Rio Grande, the *Rio Bravo,* Alec could feel summer coming on the country, sure. It was hot from the moment the sun cleared the Sandias in the morning—the day reached a fiery peak at mid-afternoon when the sun lay in the west, its rays pouring slantwise on the country like molten brass.

At first he and Alfredo were in a valley, where summer had a certain heavy steaminess. They often rode along *acequias,* running silvery with water from the river. Along their banks were cottonwoods so old and full of warts they might have been there from the days of Coronado, drawing up water with their deep roots, greening out their round coin leaves, while locusts and cicadas buzzed and clattered in their high crowns.

Upon the irrigated fields where hay was putting up its green stems through sheets of water, red-winged blackbirds preened and bathed. Men with shovels stood under wide sombreros, watching the waters spreading wide. In pastures, livestock munched the new grass, clustered near water or in the cover of the trees, content in the freshness of the young season, but knowing a need to balance the heavy fire of the sun. In such houses as they passed, people kept themselves behind their cool adobe walls, doors open to the moving air.

In a day or two they left the valley, reaching toward higher ground. Here the grass was burned and brown, giving out a dry rustle as they passed, reaching across the level benches and broken mesas until the line between it and the milk sky seemed indefinite and lost.

Save for the nearby Sandias, the mountains were that way, too—so far off they seemed to be of smoke, and in the heated air having the bluish color of iron heated in a forge. At dawn, though, they would come alive with early color, and at evening they seemed to glow with reds and lavenders, as if they had some secret, inner life that a man could only guess at.

It was at these sundowns that you came to think the Indians might be right in worshiping the sun and soil, the small running waters in the earth, granting them a power that must be sought with drums and dancing. It did not matter there were padres living with them, teaching Christian ways. In the evenings, when the far-off mountains stirred with their living fires, the heathen gods were real.

Big it was, this country, of such a reach and stretch that the mind was apt to groan to try to measure it in miles, so that you came to look at it the way an Indian might do, and think in days, or in *jornadas*.

Yet for all that the land never seemed to change, that they never seemed to make a yard upon it, still the country altered as they advanced. No more than a couple of days had passed before the distant mountains put aside their cloaks of misty vapor and took substance. A new range bent to meet them, high and reaching, green and blue with fir and spruce and pine, and beyond the timber line rose the naked spine where nothing grew, save moss and such.

This was the backbone of the Rockies. Just to see the mountains in their mass was cause enough to give a lift to Alec's heart. And when he neared them enough to make out the contours of the valleys and the forests, of the ridges and the hidden parks of aspen, he began to feel the way a man might feel when he beheld his natural country for the first time.

One evening they crossed the long *bajada* north of Santa Fe and came out on a ridge and looked down on a fine valley. It ran off east toward the shoulders of the mountains, grassy and winding. A little creek broke from the foothills, creating fields and pastures in the level bottoms. Along the water there were trees that moved their heads with the evening breeze, and here and there the golden glow of dying sunlight glinted on the binder in adobe bricks.

Alec and Alfredo had ridden all these days avoiding known trails, but here a trail led down across a valley, among fine trees and close against the water.

Alfredo nodded at it, smiling as he turned to look at Alec. He moved his hand.

"Well, *amigo,* here we are," he said.

"That way?" Alec said. "Along that trail?"

"*Si,*" Alfredo said. "Yes, that one. That is the one. It is the trail to home."

CHAPTER SIXTEEN

WHENEVER he thought of it later, Alec always felt that his first week or ten days at Alfredo's place set some kind of mark in his life for lazy living. According to Alfredo, the "house was his," and he was not allowed to raise even a finger while he was a guest in it. All that was expected of him was that he take the sun the live-long day, sleep well and hard at night, and eat the enormous meals prepared for him by Maria, Alfredo's wife.

For sheer indolence, it surpassed in some ways even the week at Pike's; for here the drowsy order of the passing days was not disturbed by any nagging worry about troopers on their trail, or by the wariness occasioned by the presence of a girl who so unsettled him.

In this mountain country, where even the Spanish tongue was of an ancient dialect, the mind had to reach to think of soldiers coming. And, unless he thought of her deliberately, even the girl began to belong to some old and half-forgotten time.

Everything was slow and timeless here—change, if any, came by the moods of nature rather than by men's work. In a certain sense Alec came to see it as a lost place, bypassed and forgotten by the restless westerings and seekings that held to known and traveled ways. The even tenor of the years had left it much as it had been in the days of the *conquistadores*.

Alfredo's place was like that, old and of a definite pattern in its ways. When asked of it, Alfredo was himself hard put to say how long his family had been grazing stock upon these hillsides, how long they had been raising hay and other crops along the bottoms, which of his kin had put the willow trees to root beside the water, and which had set the cottonwoods down beside the rambling adobe house, or how many generations might have come and gone since they had held the grant.

"It came from Carlos Segundo," he said to Alec once, and then shrugged. "Who knows? *Quien sabe*, eh?"

They were up in the burial ground beside the old adobe church. It was strange to Alec to think that any Spanish king had ever granted land in such a place as this. But looking at it another way, even the strangeness was fitting, for only the Spanish could have been here long enough to settle, and the graves bore out this truth.

"See, that is my father there," Alfredo said. "He was killed at Apache Canyon when the *gringos* came. He fought for Armijo, when Kearney took the land from Mexico." Alfredo spat on the earth, an extension of his thoughts about Armijo. "If Armijo could be said to fight," he added. "It is charity to allow it."

It was barren ground they stood in while Alfredo spoke about his father and the sorry governor, Armijo. Some of the graves had crosses, and others were too old to have them any more. The crosses were of wood, and some of the newer ones had scraps of colored paper fastened to them. A few of them had names upon them, too, painted, or inset with nailheads. But most had stood out in the weather far too long, so that even the nailheads had dissolved to streaks of brown rust.

Still, Alfredo knew them.

"Over there is my father's father," he went on. "He fought in the war with Spain, when Mexico became a nation in her own right. He died long ago, when I was still a child, a *nino*. Sometimes I can hardly remember what he looked like, but I can hear his voice. I remember him well enough, what he was like. A teller of tales, he was. He often held me on his knees and talked to me of *brujas*—witches—if you please. They were said to live in the mountains, and I remember being afraid of the mountains for a long time. I remember the goat smell, too, for he was a keeper of goats."

Alfredo laughed, wagging his head at the childish memories.

"Goats and witches—they are said to be the devil's business. Strange things to remember of a person, but he was a strange old man."

Alec looked upon the ground where Alfredo's father's father lay. The wooden cross was tilting, and was worn so badly as to seem a sliver now. He could not imagine what the old man might have looked like, but Alfredo's talk of goats and witches gave a sense of life.

"And over there is the father of my father's father. That little low one, almost into the earth now, so old it is. He died before my time—I can't think how many years have passed. But I know many things about him, though these were told to me. Perhaps I took them with my mother's milk—who knows? But I know them all my life, so that I often feel that only a part of him is gone, that a part is living still. It is that way with them all, you understand?"

There were other graves of men, women, and little children. Alfredo knew them all, though some had lain so long that they no longer had a cross above them, and over a few the caliche mound had been so worn by rain and sun and wind that the earth was nearly level. A cemetery was a place of sadness, but Alfredo hardly sounded sad. In fact, he sounded cheerful as he passed from grave to grave and told his little stories over the mounds.

Perhaps it was Alfredo's smiling, joking comment in this place, his lack of solemnity, that gave Alec cause to feel the way he did. Perhaps it was the fact that nothing here had changed since even the oldest of these dead had been put into the ground. Whatever it was, the fact of death was blunted here, and like Alfredo, Alec could see how the ancient ones might seem to linger still, in this place of the past.

They were sitting before the casa toward the close of an afternoon. It was late enough for the mountains to begin to show their evening colors. Down below them in the bottoms cattle grazed on the *vega,* and new alfalfa stood up green and bright in a field beyond. The sun was at that angle at which the trees all radiated light, as if they glowed within themselves. Coming from the hills, the water had the brilliance of polished metal winding through the valley.

"See how the fields are separated," Alfredo said, and Alec looked below them at the fields.

He had not thought very much of them as separate fields before. Long and narrow, they ran over the bottoms, divided by fencelines made of brush or rock, or whatever had come to hand.

Alfredo said when Alec asked him why the fields were laid out that way, "They tell of the length of time we have been here in this valley and of the fertility of my people." He laughed. "Listen—in the beginning the land was all open. When the first ones came there were no fences, no walls. Then the first ones died, and the land was given to the sons, each of an equal portion. It was long ago, more than a hundred years, more than a hundred and fifty years. Then the sons died, the land was split again among sons of theirs. More fences were put up; more stone taken from the creek for walls. Look at them. You can see how long."

Alec looked at the divided land and was taken with a sense of time. Each of the fields spoke of a passing generation, a lifetime from infancy to manhood, and then to old age and death. The fields went up the valley for as far as he could see, row upon row, until the foothills took them in. In a way they spoke of change, but of a patterned changelessness, too, and once again Alec had the feeling of the old ones still living here, and not as ghosts, either.

"Yes, I see, all right," he said. "It's been going on a while." He laughed. "You keep this up, there'll be no room for crops."

"Yes," Alfredo said. "There is that danger. Perhaps it would be better that our men were geldings."

He smiled, spreading his hands upon his knees. "Or that we tear the fences down for plowing room. I think we might do that one day." He laughed, putting his hands before him, as though to warm them at a fire. "Still, it is the custom. It is the old way."

Out behind the casa was a hive-shaped oven, made of adobe blocks. On certain days Maria baked her bread in it, and once Alec asked her why it hadn't been built in the kitchen.

Alfredo's wife was near his own age. She was well rounded and had a smiling face and very black, wavy hair. Often she would dust her face with gypsum powder, and in the evening, when the work of the day was done and they were sitting by the fire, she would smoke *cigarros*.

"Why?" she now said of the oven, smiling up at him. "Would it make the bread taste better?"

"Why, I don't know," Alec said, for he had never thought of the matter in that light, but only the convenience of having the oven in the house. "I like it fine enough the way it is."

"Yes," she said, still smiling at him as she worked. "To make bread this way gives it a fine taste. This oven bakes it just right. It is the old way."

Often, too, she would grind com for her tortillas on an old *metate* made of lava, using a heavy *mano* to crush the kernels into meal. Sometimes she would spend the whole of the day upon her knees, and though she sang and talked he would feel sorry for her. The valley had no mill where com and flour could be ground, but he knew better now than to ask her why. It was the custom. That was sufficient reason.

It was a place of custom and of old ways. Alec learned enough to know that some of the ways were bad, or wasteful, and that often they made more work than a thing might need for doing. Still, there was a comfort in them, too, the sense of doing a thing in a manner of proven worth, knowing that what you did would be preserved by those who might come after you. This underlying thought appealed to him, and more and more it pleased him that he had come here to this valley in the high and silent mountains. Ever since he was a kid, it was the kind of country that he had had in mind.

CHAPTER SEVENTEEN

"HEY, *amigo,*" Alfredo said one evening on returning from a day off in the valley somewhere, "sleep well tonight—tomorrow we ride. In the early dawn."

They were sitting by the fire before the house. The night was dark, but at this altitude the stars were very bright and luminous. It was cool, too.

"Troopers coming?" Alec said. In his mind was a vision of a column coming north, and the thought surprised him with its suddenness, though there was no reason why it should. He had lived so long with flight holding the foremost claim upon his thoughts that the feel of the hunted should have been second nature to him now, even up here in this place.

"No, no," Alfredo laughed. He patted Alec on the shoulder. "I want to show you something. Something nice."

"What's that?"

"Well, you want a place to live, don't you? I know an old man who has some valley land where you can build your home. It is good land, and there are water rights, too; that is important."

"A home begins with a woman, *alma mia,*" Maria said. She winked at Alec. "Call it a house—be accurate."

"How can it be either one until it is built?" Alfredo said. "Tell me that, if you can. Be sensible."

"It is all a matter of terms," Maria said. "You think of a roof and walls—I think of what goes on within them. The difference is in the name you give them."

Alfredo raised his eyes as if to ask God's witness to this woman's nonsense.

"Maria, *mia*, I simply try to tell him of this place I know of. Why can't you let me do that?"

"Tell him," Maria said. "By all means, tell him. But please be accurate—there is always a woman in a home."

Alec felt uncomfortable to hear this woman talk pop up. He felt uneasy, as he had when talk of Ruth had come up at Pike's, but this was different, too. He would like to forget about her now, and it didn't help to have this kind of discussion remind him of her.

"Where did you find this place?" he asked to put an end to it. "Nearby, is it?"

"No, but not too far, either. It is up at the head of the valley, here—a day's ride, perhaps. It has been some years since I was there, but I remember it. The valley narrows some, but there is room enough for winter hay and plenty of water. In the mountain meadows above, there is fine free grass and open range. The cows have only to eat."

Alec raised his coffee cup and drank from it. The sound of what Alfredo said was good, but he had thought of such a place too long, shaped it too much in his mind, to let himself get fired up too quickly.

"How do you know the place can be had?" he asked.

"This old man of whom I speak, who owns it, lives here in the valley—down this way." Alfredo waved his arm at some indefinite point in the dark. "He has never used that land up there. Until late years the Indians were troublesome. Now he is too old, nor has he any sons. I talked with him today. He would be willing to deal."

Alec began to visualize it in his mind—the high head of the valley, where the water ran blue-black in its cold and purity. At this time of year there would be flowers in the meadows, and below the naked peaks would be a beard of green timber.

He would need money, though. The range was free, but the bottoms and the water rights would cost.

"Would he be willing to take his pay in beef? Or take the market price at selling time?"

"We spoke of that," Alfredo said, and then he gave his soft laugh. It was as if he were stringing the deal out like a reata, yard by yard, so as to milk it of all the pleasure it might give him. "Yes, we spoke of that—he is old, and his needs are small. He is agreeable." He spread his hands. "What more can you ask?"

"Not much," Alec said. "Only to have a look at it." He felt his jaw strain with the wideness of his grin, and he could see the valley once again, the bold peaks and painted flowers in the meadows. Almost, he could see a stand of hay.

He took another drink, and set the cup down.

"You're some fixer, ain't you?"

Alfredo didn't speak, but only shrugged his shoulders while the firelight glistened on his teeth.

"Perhaps you fixed a woman for him, too," Maria said. She blew out a puff of smoke and watched it rise. "Do not forget what I said. A home begins with a woman."

In the morning they rode through the winding valley toward the mountains, climbing slowly. This was the Sangre de Cristo range—the Blood of Christ—and after they got closer Alec could make out the different belts of trees, and once or twice, above the timberline, he saw the marks of snow upon the northern faces of the barren peaks.

For a long while the valley remained as it was around Alfredo's place. Along the water were the same trees, green with summer and old. Deep among them now and then, he could make out a house, built so as to have the benefit of shade, for even at this height the sun at the peak of a summer day was warm.

Sometimes they held to the trail, at other times they rode along the water. The fields they passed were high and thick with crops; most of the stock was in the hills above, moving dots which would be sheep or cattle. Once they passed a herd of goats upon a nearby hillside in the care of an elderly man, who nodded gravely as they passed.

By late afternoon, they were well up toward the head of the valley, and far beyond that lower part of it where all the little farms and pastures were. There were few fences here and only now and then a house. The trees were changing some along the water; the cottonwoods were giving way to sycamore and alder, and up on the nearby hills—hills which rose more steeply now—there began to be some pine and fir among the juniper and *piñon*.

"We are getting there, *amigo*," Alfredo said in a while. "It is beginning to look as I remember it."

They drew up along the water. Alfredo put his hand on the cantle to support himself and turned to look about him.

"You know how it is," he said as he looked around, seeking out landmarks. "You see a place and you remember things, and then you go away. Then, when you come back, you have to look again. But we are almost there now. See if you can find an old burn on the mountain."

Alec moved his eyes across the mountain while Alfredo talked. The shadows of the summer clouds lay dark in fields of sunlight, but one of the shadowed places had a stand of silver wires in it, as of young aspen shining in the light. After a fire, aspen always seeded first.

"There it is," he said, and raised his arm. "Not far either."

"Ah," Alfredo said. "Indeed. That is the one, all right. The place we look for is just below it."

They went on again, and Alec felt an excitement in him now. He felt a curious sense of pride and ownership, and rode very slowly to be sure to see all the land—noting the slope of the bottoms toward the water, gauging the fall of the creek so as to know the height of the head for irrigation. Every now and then he would stop to measure the growth of grass, getting down to run the long stems through his fingers. It was all heavy grama, blue and black together, and looked as if it never had been grazed before. This was the head of the valley, and there were meadows flowing outward toward the creases in the mountains, lifting to the very shoulders of the peaks, the edge of deep timber. Across them lay shoals of columbine and yarrow, shooting star and monkshood, and other wildflowers glowing in the dying sunlight.

Alfredo said, "This is how I remember it. How fine the grass lies. Do you like it?"

"Yes, I like it," Alec said, knowing the words did not come up to what he felt, but knowing, too, that hardly any would.

He was aware of speaking quietly, as though to keep a tight rein on his feelings. It was hard for him to remember how long he had thought of such a place as this, a place that had whatever a man could ask in reason—water, timber, grass. Far back in his memory the vision traveled, back even to those childhood days when his mind had first been fired by the wandering mountain men.

And here it all was, just as he had carried it in his mind all these years.

He and Alfredo were walking now, leading their horses. At the creek, they stopped to let the animals water.

"See that little bench?" Alfredo said, moving his hand. "A corral would go there, underneath it, if you liked it. The height is right for it."

Alec looked across the blue-black water at the bench. It was guarded by the overhang against the downward currents of the night, and against the winds of winter. Moreover, it was flat ground, and near enough to water to make it possible to let a little ditch run through it.

"Yes," he said in a moment, "a corral would go there good enough."

"And over there," Alfredo said and raised his arm again, "over there would make a good hay field. It is level and has a proper size."

Alec followed the motion of Alfredo's arm, and it was as Alfredo said. The field lay upstream a ways. It held level for a number of acres, and irrigating it would be easy. Between it and the overhang there was even a little sink, or hollow, where he might have a pond.

"Yes, I see it," Alec said, and he saw more than just the level ground. He could see a horse or two behind the fresh-peeled poles, nuzzling water with their silky noses while they whisked their tails. Sniffing at the air, he came close to smelling growing hay upon the breeze, and he could see it, green and waving, stretching up for cutting.

"Then you will have to have a house," Alfredo said. "Or, is it a home? We should have Maria here—she would tell us."

"I think a lean-to's what I need for now," Alec said. "By the time I get the rest laid out, the ditches dug and all, winter'll be coming off the mountain."

"Yes, there is that to think of—it comes early up this way. Still, you could choose a place for a house. That would do no harm."

"No, it wouldn't do no harm."

But now that he thought of it, he felt a fussiness come over him. Such a place as he would like to build, such a place as would be right to bring a woman to—and there would be a woman coming to it one day—could be no ordinary shack, no boar's nest, such as he was used to in these past years. It had to be a special thing; it had to be of a certain build, and stand in a certain place—in all ways, it had to be just right.

"There is room beneath the overhang," Alfredo said. "It would go beside the corral. Or, over there beside the hay field. That is a fine place there, flat and open—you will never be cramped for space."

"Nor for wind in winter, either," Alec said.

"Ah, the wind, yes," Alfredo said. He tugged at his mustachios. Then he raised his head, using his chin to point beyond. "What about those trees up there? From here it looks like a fine grove."

Alec had seen the grove himself, and knew it for the right place. Spreading over the ground for half an acre, it stood back beyond the floods of spring, but not so far that water wasn't handy. Walking toward it, he could see the limber pine and foxtail pine which gave it height and would serve to break the wind. Lower down was a growth of juniper and chokecherry and other bushy shrubs.

As they neared the grove he could see motion through the trees. This turned out to be a buck deer, a tall and beautiful creature, lithe and strong. It was not afraid, for they stood downwind from it. At the water, it dipped its muzzle in to drink, then crossed to the other side.

Browsing, it went slowly onward, unaware of them. It came into a meadow now and nosed among the wildflowers. All about, the valley lay in evening shadow, but over beyond, there was a patch of dying sunlight, and when the deer came into it its coat turned bright and alive. Of a sudden, Alec's mind turned on the memory of the doe and fawn that he had seen that early morning in the Guadalupes when he and Stone were heading for the Mescalero. The time seemed long ago to him, but the memory was very real. A time had passed since he had thought consciously of Stone and Clint and Roy, and of the bloody wildness of those days, but now this deer had brought them back.

It was queer and strange that they should come to mind with such a vividness, up here in this isolated valley, up here in this fine place. It was as if they showed themselves to say that nothing had been finished, after all. Were he superstitious, he might even take it as a warning of some kind.

CHAPTER EIGHTEEN

FOR ALEC, the month and more that followed upon their finding of the high valley were the finest time of his life, for he was giving substance to a dream that he had had for a long while. At no other time that he could think of in his grown years was he so free to put his thoughts and work upon matters of his own choosing. The simple fact of being able to shape his life as he might wish to shape it was a triumph in itself, and now he had the added pleasure of beginning a thing of his own stamp, of building according to his own wishes, with the hope in mind of watching what he built grow throughout his life, and passing it on to such as might come after him.

Having worked for others in the times now gone, this was a strange and novel thing to him. It seemed to give a new and deeper meaning to existence, and he was able to understand a little better his father's pride in their old place on the plains. Even now in memory—and memory was often kind to faults—the old place wasn't much. He remembered wind blowing endlessly, drought threatening and, often as not, the grass would go to sand.

Still, whatever the faults the place had had, it never lessened in his father's eyes. It was all his own, the dreams he had of it were his, and Comanches were the only ones could bring it to an end.

There was a lot of work to be done, and most of the time it was his to do alone, but Alfredo sometimes helped. Sometimes a nephew of Alfredo's named Hernando, a tall, gangling boy, would give him a day or two. Hernando was slow but he was strong, and when there were ditches to be dug, and leveling to be done, and raw earth to be graded, and timbers to be hewn, strength was welcome, slow or not. Still, Alec worked mostly alone. A man could work until he shook all over with fatigue if he had a dream to beckon him.

As he had no money for implements or tools, or any means to get them up there to the valley head, he had to beg or borrow them. From an elderly widow, a *curandera,* who had no momentary need for them, he borrowed a pair of mules. From an uncle of Alfredo's, he got a flat-bed wagon, and from various others in the lower valley he was able to get the loan of a plow, shovels, axes, hammers, and such other things he needed.

In a way it was an inconvenience, for the loan of the mules would cost him time to plow the *curandera's* fields when he was done with them; and the use of the wagon would cost him time to get the uncle's hay crop in when it was cut, and there were various other strings.

Too, it was grinding on his pride to borrow things, but even pride could bend a little to a dream.

The work went slowly, but it went on. The corral was finished by the first of August, the poles cut out of jackpines hewn above the valley on the mountain, and carried in the wagon to the bench beneath the overhang, where they were lashed and nailed into place. It was hard to say why he wanted to build that first, ahead of other things, except that he was a horseman, and a horseman put his riding stock before himself.

After that he worked upon his hay fields, leveling and dragging them, running his ditches through them on the proper gradient, building a little dam and headgate out of rock and mortar in the creek, so as to draw the water off when needed. The season was too late to seed this year, but he wanted to have the fields ready for the following spring. The ditches and the fields, together with the headgate, took a month to do the way he liked them, and August was nearly over when he finished them.

Sometimes there were setbacks, too, delays to bother him. Once a storm heaved over the mountain of an afternoon. While he sat beneath the little lean-to watching it, the downpour ruined a stack of blocks that he had molded of adobe and set to cure. Another time, an axle on the wagon snapped, and he was two days shaping and fitting another to replace it.

Yet a man could stand defeats and failures, too, so long as there was still the dream.

It was in September when he cleared the ground to build his house, and when the dream began to have that special vividness of being realized. A man could have a place, a grazing land, a pasture, he could plow a field and sow it, he could rig a dam to carry water to it, but still his work had a temporary quality until he built his house. All the rest could be wiped away by a winter storm or heavy springtime flood, and in a year the land might look as though no man had touched it.

But the building of a house was different. The building of a house meant that a man would stay to fight the floods, if there were floods, and that he'd cut the losses of the winter freeze, if there were losses. It meant a willing binding of himself to whatever fortunes might befall his land. It meant that roots were going down. It spoke out of a settled quality, a permanence. It was a declaration of intent to stay, to cast his lot with the land until such time as he no longer had the life or breath in him to cast his lot with anything.

Moreover, it meant a cutting of ties with the past. And perhaps it was the knowing of that that brought the past so quickly to his mind these days. It was as if he must examine it, must poke among its relics and its memories, to see what implications it might hold for him, before he let it go.

Perhaps he might have let it go at that, no matter he knew he might be wanted, still, and no matter the deer he often saw brought up the face of Stone to think about. Perhaps he might have gone on building, planning, living as he'd always wished to, in this isolated place—if Pike had only sayed in Bernalillo. But Pike would not stay put. In the middle of September, he came north, and with him came the past and all its complications, too.

It was one of the times when Alec was coming down to get Hernando's help. The walls were raised, but the *vigas* that he'd cut upon the mountain were too heavy to place alone. Moreover, the time was near to do the plowing in payment for the mules; it would save the time of another trip to do the plowing now.

It was evening when he reached Alfredo's place. From a distance, as he came along the lower valley, he could see the little fire out in front of it. In a while he could make out some people, too, gathered about with smokes and coffee, but he did not see Pike until he came to the fire.

Then Pike stood beside the fire, grinning.

"Well," Alec said, and then he smiled. He wiped his hands along his jeans as he came forward. "Well," he said again. "It's you. How in hell are you?"

"Fine," Pike said, "fine. I'm fine." He took a poke at Alec with his fist, and Alec poked him back, while Maria and Alfredo laughed and hooted. "By God, you look all right, Alec—what's more, you look like you been doin' honest work, too."

"It's work, all right," Alec said. "I guess it's honest. I hope you can say the same."

"Well, I'm workin', sure enough," Pike said. "More'n I ever thought I would. Jud took out on me a couple of weeks ago—I got no choice about it." He laughed again, and raised his chin at the tethered mules beneath the tree. "Plowin', are you? God, I never thought to see you plowin' anything."

"You ain't yet," Alec said, "but stick around. I'll be plowin' tomorrow some."

"Yes, he is a fine plowboy," Alfredo said. "Tomorrow he plows for the widow Mercedes and you will see him then. He has a certain touch."

"Is that so?" Pike said. "By God, I can believe it." He stepped aside and bent his head as if to study Alec. "Be damned if he don't look it, some—he's even got a little of that hunch, the plowboy's hunch! He's gettin' to be a regular grayback, was I asked."

"Not that you was asked about it," Alec said, still smiling, full of the sudden gladness at seeing Pike. "It's the dirt that does it, anyway. Go on, sit down, while I get washed."

He turned to the basin on the bench beneath the wall of the casa, pouring the water out of the pitcher and sloshing it over his face and arms. When he got back to the fire Maria came out of the house with a plate of tortillas. He sat, and they were quiet for a moment while they ate, that quietness of taking stock that follows upon the whoop and holler that men will make upon first meeting after a time apart. Giving a look at him from time to time between the mouthfuls of tortillas, it seemed to Alec that Pike was still the same. Perhaps because he'd felt a change in himself, for he thought to see one in Pike—months had passed since he had had a look at him—but Pike was still the same, young and kid-like, full of fun and foolishness.

"You spoke of Jud a minute ago," Alec said when he had washed the first tortilla down.

Pike nodded. "Uh-huh. Like I said, he just left. I guess he'd thought about going long enough, and talked of it. With me come back, he saw his chance and took it."

Alec thought about the girl, Ruth Hagan, wondering if she'd gone with him, or stayed, or what. He wanted to ask, but just knowing that was enough to keep him still and wary.

Instead he said, "I guess I ain't the only grayback in the country any more. I don't suppose you're sittin' in your dooryard like a don these days, free an' easy while the others work."

"No, I ain't, that's sure," Pike said, smiling and scowling, both. "And I ain't sure I like it either. To tell the truth, I had part of a mind to go with him."

"You weren't talkin' that way in the Guadalupes," Alec said.

"No, and the work was plenty far off, too," Pike said.

"Maybe you're runnin' out yourself, then, coming up here," Alec said. "You lookin' for a change? I got a roof needs puttin' on."

Pike laughed, leaning back on his elbows. "Things ain't that bad. I was only kiddin' a little, anyway." Still smiling, Pike hunched up again and took a swallow of coffee. "I just come to bring the news, is all."

"What kind of news is that?"

"Well, I saw Lorenzo," Pike said. And then he let it hang.

"Oh-ho," Alfredo said. "Lorenzo?"

Alec felt a caution come over him. He couldn't think why this should be, but it was there, sudden and unbidden. It was as if any news, whatever it might be, that Pike would bring up here among these quiet valleys would be an intrusion.

He began to roll a cigarette.

"Where at did you see Lorenzo, Pike?" he asked.

"In Albuquerque," Pike said. "I ran into him when I went down the other day. He was over buying store-goods, and seeing the doings."

"Ah, the doings," Alfredo said. "The fiesta. They are celebrating the name-day of the city, Alec. We should go to that." He laughed. "If we don't mind hanging."

"If we don't mind hanging," Alec agreed. Then, to Pike, he said, "What did Lorenzo have in mind?"

"Oh, it was about the fire, you know, the one at Anders' place, and about the inquest on the hold-up of the stage, and all that—then about Stone, too, and them Indians he had."

Pike drank out of his coffee cup and set it down.

"You know, I'm kind of glad you kicked me home before that happened, Alec. Not that I wouldn't have gone—I wanted to, as you remember. Still, now, I'm just as glad I didn't."

"I'm glad you didn't, too, Pike. And I've wished aplenty we'd stayed out of it. Had we done some good, it might be different, but we didn't. It was all a waste."

Alec sealed his cigarette with his tongue and put it into his mouth, lighting it with a stick from the fire.

"What'd he have to say about it, anyway—Lorenzo?"

"Well, the soldiers are in it now, for one thing, the bluebellies—they're running things. The local law ain't in it any more."

"That was bound to happen," Alec said. "You can't turn Indians loose, without you get the soldiers on your neck."

"It looks that way, all right," Pike said. "Anyway, they're on the hunt, have been ever since. According to Lorenzo, they killed a number at the fire, and others later, up on the Mescalero. They're about done with them, I guess. Still, there's Stone."

"Broke free, did he—Stone?" And he knew that it would be inevitable that Stone should. Now it seemed that all his recent thoughts of Stone, up there in the high valley, when he had seen the deer, and at other times, had been leading up to this—had in their own way confirmed the fact that his past still held him in its shadow. For all his carelessness and dumbness, Stone had always had a talent for saving his own skin.

"Yes, he broke free, all right," Pike said. "And they been huntin' him ever since—him and Clint. Roy was killed, though. They got him at the fire down at Anders'."

Neither was that surprising, Alec thought. If any of them should have got it, it was Roy. Roy was always a little slow to catch onto a thing. It was easy for Alec to see in his mind how Roy's eyes spread at a problem and how the thoughts moved slowly through them.

"What about us?" he said in a minute, and then he saw Pike fiddling with his cup and knew what the answer would be. It was a foolish thing to ask.

"Well, I'm out of it, I guess," Pike said. "If Lorenzo's got it straight. And he didn't say about Alfredo, either." Pike slowed, as if to soften what was coming next, but Alec spoke before he could go any further with it.

"I know—I'm elected." He laughed, although he hardly felt it as a laugh. "Me and Stone and Clint. By hell, that's something, ain't it?"

"Ah, what the hell, it's only what Lorenzo said. He could be wrong. But you was down at Anders'—they know that."

"I, too, was there," Alfredo said. "How can it be that I have not the honor of being named?" He slapped his thigh, as if he took it as a slight to be ignored. "How can they say that he was there, and I was not? Tell me that, if you will."

Pike shrugged, giving his head a jerk. "You wasn't seen, is all, I guess. But Alec was. Somebody got a look at him somehow. Could be one of the Stanton troopers knew him."

Alec nodded, knowing the possibility of such a thing.

"That could be," he said. "I've known a few of 'em off and on, over the years."

"But, what of the stage?" Alfredo said, as if he felt there still might be a chance for his name to figure there. "Was I not at the stage?"

"Maybe it's on account this other thing is bigger than the stage," Pike said. "The troopers wouldn't hold no stage holdup to be equal of an Indian massacre. Was it local law alone, it might be different, but it ain't no local law no more. I guess they maybe lumped them both together now. Anyway, the only name the inquest settled on was Stone's—the driver remembered the general look of him."

Alec took a pull at his smoke and let it go.

"Likely he recalled that pistol in his tail," he said. "I'd be plenty watchful of the man that done it."

"I guess he did, at that," Pike said. "And he sat on the inquest."

"He did?" Alec said. Then he laughed. "Good for him."

It was something, anyhow, to have had Lorenzo at the inquest, too, pulling wires, keeping their names from turning up. Not that it made much difference to himself, but Pike was in the clear now all the way, and Alfredo, too, looked to be shed of it. However it went for him, he could be grateful for that much, at least.

It was later now. The fire had diminished, sinking into its bed of coals, and Alfredo had built it up again. The coffeepot had emptied, and Maria had made more and set it on a flat stone near the fire to keep its heat. The night had turned cooler.

"Alec?"

It was Pike, and Alec raised his head.

"What is it?" Alec said, and wondered what could be coming next. He felt dull and heavy, the way he always felt when he was being ridden by the past.

Pike smiled in a way that said he understood about the dullness and the heaviness in Alec.

"It ain't nothin' to do with Stone or with the troopers, Alec. I only wanted to ask you something. Still, I don't guess I'd be askin' if I hadn't seen Lorenzo—knowin' I'm in the clear makes it different. I got you to thank for that, I guess."

"I don't know why you should," Alec said, and then he gave a snort. "You only needed to have what you already knew was laid out for you."

"Yah—maybe," Pike said. "Still, I owe you thanks. Was I still wanted like—" He stopped and his face grew red.

"Like me," Alec said, rubbing the earth with his hand. "Go on."

"Well, yeah, like you," Pike said. He laughed self-consciously and hunched around on the hide he sat on. "What I mean is, I wouldn't be askin' was I wanted, still. That's what I mean."

"All right," Alec said, and now he wondered why he should feel irritated. It was the way things weighed on him, or the way that Pike would sometimes maul a thing.

"Well, what I wanted to ask," Pike said, leaning forward, "was about that girl. Ruth, you know? The kin of Jud that yondered off again?"

Alfredo had been quiet for some time, but now he glanced at Alec and laughed softly. "Oh-ho," he said. "The feisty one. Do you remember her, *amigo?*"

But Alec paid no heed to what Alfredo said. He was watching Pike, and already he knew what Pike was going to ask.

"What about her, Pike?" he said, and he wondered if he sounded loud.

"Well, you know she's all alone now," Pike said. "You know she ain't got anyone out here. And you know she's got no money, either."

Pike began to slow in what he said, and then as if he must be primed to move again, he took a swallow of coffee.

"What I meant to ask was, should I ask to marry her."

It was just what Alec thought that Pike was going to ask, and now it made him angry. Pike's hemming and hawing over it gave plenty of warning of its coming, but it angered him, anyway. He hardly knew why he should feel this way, but Pike sure hadn't any right to ask him that. Now that he thought about it, Pike was always asking help on things he ought to decide himself. If it wasn't one thing, by hell, it was another, and enough to make you spit. It was time Pike grew up.

"What you askin' me for?" Alec said. He sounded rough, and knew it, but he didn't care.

"I don't mean to make you sore," Pike said. "I know how you feel about her—how you don't get on with her. I just thought I'd ask, is all."

"I ain't sore about it," Alec said, which made him sorer, but held rein on his temper better this time. "But I can't see how I can help you any."

"Well, I ain't much at women, Alec. Marryin' up is a pretty big thing, and a man can make good use of all the views that he can get."

"A man who gives advice must share the blame if things go wrong," Alfredo said.

"You would like to give it, though," Maria said. Then, to Pike, she said, "Are you buying a cow? Do you want to form a committee to select her? Men!" She blew out a puff of smoke.

"Ain't nobody's view counts but your own, Pike," Alec said. "You got to live with her."

"Well, I like her well enough. Her cookin's plenty good, and I guess you know she does for a person when he's sick or something." He let his eyes fall to the cigarette he held between his fingers. "I just thought I'd ask, is all."

"Well, that's your answer, ain't it?" Alec said; and then some perverse thing took hold of him, some crazy thing he couldn't help, which made him say, "Go and marry her, if you like—go ahead and ask her. You could have worked that out yourself."

"Why—" Pike said, and then he smiled as if a new thought had come to him. "Why, I guess that's so. Thanks, Alec—thanks a lot. I don't know why I shouldn't ask her."

It was then that Alec felt the weariness, a weariness beyond all telling, coming over him. For a moment he came close to wishing Pike had stayed in Bernalillo with his news, his revelations. Then he was ashamed to think that way, for he and Pike were *companeros* for a long while. Later he would feel it even stronger, the sense of shame—for, though he did not know it then, that evening at Alfredo's was the last he ever saw of Pike.

CHAPTER NINETEEN

I T WAS STRANGE how fall could sneak upon a country, Alec thought, coming unnoticed and unannounced, in the way of a cat that stalks a mouse. There would be quiet and mellow days, days of an even warmth; chimney smoke of an evening would rise straight and blue; at night, the moon was harvest color, deeply yellow, going to orange while the air had a coolness. But if there was a chill it came upon the country in the darkest hours, when everyone was sleeping, so that in the morning when you wakened and could see the change of color in the highlands, you would be surprised.

Fall warned of winter, spring of summer—no season gave notice of fall.

High up in his upper valley where Alec labored on his roof, he could make out these changes working on the many faces of the mountains. In the summer you would have to look to know the way the green of aspen differed from the green of pine or fir. But now the aspen groves were changing; first the butter yellow of the surprising early chill, then the deeper gold of nightly frost, until the whole of the mountain glowed with pockets of dying light.

Scattered among them here and there against the level green of conifers, there would be maple trees and sumac; for a time they had the look of iron that had laid out for a while, weathered and rusty, but soon the rustiness was gone and they turned red and bright, like raw wounds needing dressing.

Lower, the junipers would have their summer berries going blue, and *piñon* would ready their crops of nuts, with the squirrels putting up a fuss and quarrel. Grazing horses drifted restlessly.

The air was crisper in the mornings when he awoke, and sometimes there appeared a glistening on the high peaks, as if a skim of snow had fallen on them in the night. Down along the lower valley the cottonwoods were burning with a brassy flame, and hanging from the *vigas* there began to be long *ristras* of scarlet chili peppers, set to cure. In the evenings the smell of *piñon* smoke and incense cedar had a special fragrance; all the deer were in the blue, and the antlers on the bucks were getting hard and sharp for fighting.

It was the finest time of the year, fall was, Alec sometimes thought—a time of taking stock, of tying down for winter, of preparing to fight.

While all the colors of the falling leaves spoke out to say it was a time of death, as well, for growing things, still the very brilliance of those colors seemed to give a promise that life would come again, just as it always had. No matter the grass would wither and some trees stand naked, it was hard to feel cast down when you could see the gay and sassy colors speaking out about that time they knew of, when the cold of winter eased, and spring would bring the new life.

Still, no matter it was the finest time, he seemed now to feel the dying side of it, the somber side.

After Pike had gone and he had done the plowing for the widow Mercedes, and come back up to the valley head to finish the work on his house, he sensed a change. The place looked different in some way. Four days was all he'd spent away, but he had the feeling of having been upon a distant journey, and of returning after many weeks or months.

He knew the source of the feeling well enough—it was Pike and the intervention of the past. In the weeks of building, the past had kept its place. His devotion to making reality of dreams and long-held hopes had made his memories of the past unsettling and unwelcome.

Sometimes they would come upon him by surprise, but in this high valley, it had not been too hard to keep them where they properly belonged, far away in another time and place. They had nothing to do with what he planned or what he built for. He could not forget them altogether, but if he worked enough and planned enough and thought enough, he could often fill his mind against them.

But Pike had changed all that. Pike had brought the past right here. Moreover, he had shown it to be as alive as it had ever been, and full of evils and dangers for him, too.

So now he was taken by uneasiness. It made no difference how he spent himself on work, how he built and planned, the past and all its meaning plagued him, unsettled him.

Sometimes he would think of Stone, and would wonder where the man was, and then he would marvel at how he had ever let himself believe that Stone was dead. In his mind's eye, he would see him sitting by the fire on the Mescalero, his heavy, meaty face dark and brooding with the brutal thoughts behind it.

Then he would think of Clint. His thoughts of Clint would always see him trailing through the forest, hunching over, searching, his face becoming sharp when he was seen and knew it. Then his hands would be about Clint's throat. There would be that knobby thing beneath his thumbs. Clint's legs would buckle, and his eyes would roll so that the whites would show.

Sometimes there were troopers riding in his mind. He would see them in the flames of Anders' place, the yellow stripes along their trousers, and hear them whooping as they came in with their sabers glinting. At other times he saw them simply riding through an unknown land, seeking, hunting, and riding always, never resting. It was a sinister thought to have, for he knew whom they were looking for.

He thought of the girl, too, despite himself. He thought of her a lot, but not of the quarrels now. These days he remembered her arms about him, and the scent of her, the moistness of her lips, the passion of her kiss—and her ultimate rejection of him, too.

It was all there, the past, crowding in on him. He had sometimes heard it said the past was dead, but it was wrong to think so. No man could run away from what he'd done or hadn't done—nor could he lessen it by choosing not to think about it.

When it came, it happened in a way he hadn't thought of; but that was the way things always happened that you had set your mind against.

That was how it was the morning he saw Alfredo coming up the valley. Alec was working on his roof when he caught sight of him.

Alfredo would not spend the whole night in the saddle out of whimsy. Nor would he hold his horse to a run against the rising grade of the valley floor for nothing.

Alec put his hammer down and waited. He could see Alfredo coming very fast, and it was like the past itself rushing up the valley floor to meet him.

Alfredo rode across the creek and Alec could see the cold, dark water shatter into brilliance in the sunlight. Overhead, the sky was rich and blue. The air was clear and bright, and in the way of mountain country in the fall, the trees and stony peaks had a clarity and nearness that could fool you. Autumn was the finest time, he thought, in any land, and now he sought to drink it in, the whole of it, while there was time, as if he knew already his time with it was at an end.

Then he looked again and saw Alfredo was trying to shout at him. Alfredo's hat was over on his neck and the horse he rode cut off in a circle while he shouted.

"What?" Alec yelled, not hearing him at first.

"There is a message from Bernalillo! Stone was there!"

"Stone?" Alec said, and a blankness took him for a second. He had thought too long of Stone among the Guadalupes and Sacramentos to have a vision of him on the Rio Grande.

"Yes, yes—Stone!" Alfredo yelled. "Stone and Clint! They have come to Bernalillo; they have killed him! Pike is dead!"

"Dead?" Alec said. It was just a word at first, a question. He looked around him—it was as if he needed some reference point outside himself to find the answer to it.

But the things he saw were strange to him—the fields, the ditches and the dam, the pole corral and creek. Even the slope of the familiar roof beneath his feet was strange.

Whatever else he knew, he knew he had no business here; not any more. He had no right to it, and he should never have come at all.

CHAPTER TWENTY

THE FIRES WERE out in the casa and in the baking oven. The loose stock had been freed to grass; the horses had been rigged and were waiting. Their saddlebags were bulging and from pommels hung heavy *morals* of food. Alfredo was already mounted, his blanket hung across his shoulders, for the early dawn was frosty. Alec was on the ground beside his sorrel mare, putting on his gunbelt and speculating on the strangeness of its weight along his leg—and of the other weight upon his mind.

Maria closed the windows and locked the door, then dropped the heavy key into the bosom of her white blouse. She was wearing a dark rebozo which fell across her bare legs when she mounted, for she rode astride.

Alfredo smiled and raised his eyebrows, and Maria looked at him and said, "It is the chill, *alma mia,* not the legs. They do not shame me yet, even at thirty-three."

Alec only grunted over this. He was against the whole idea of Maria's and Alfredo's coming, and it made no difference that they'd chewed it over most of the night.

"Serve you right if you catch your death of cold," he said. "You got no business coming along at all."

"You spoke of that before," Maria said. "It seems to me you touched upon it many times. I believe I even dreamed of it."

"So, and I meant it, too. You ought not to come along. This ain't no woman's business."

"Ha! A lot you know of woman's business," Maria said. "I go to see the girl. Someone must take care of her—she has an interesting sound. You men with your fights and brawls, could I count on you to see her? Ha!"

They were going through the dooryard under the trees, and when they reached the road Alec slowed to let Alfredo come abreast of him. It was always bad to argue with Maria—Alfredo had his own mind, too, but it didn't always seek to turn an argument upon the giver, as Maria's did.

"You ought to stay here, too, just as she should," Alec said. "You got no business coming, either."

"How can you say that, friend? Who will do the burying? Surely, there will be some burying. Perhaps I can see to the girl a little, too." Alfredo smiled. "She did not seem feisty to me."

"Then I'll drop you off where she lives," Alec said. "Go that far, if you like, but not beyond. I'm on the hunt for Stone alone."

"*Que va*," Alfredo said. "What difference does it make? He is my business, too—how can you talk that way?"

"Because you're clear of it now," Alec said. "You ain't even wanted. I guess you heard Pike tell you that—don't tell me it don't mean nothin', either."

"Ah, yes," Alfredo said. "But Pike was clear of it, too. And look at him now."

Alec had no answer to that and they rode on in silence. It was cool in the early morning and he turned the collar of his shirt against his neck. The mountains in the east were slow to let the sunlight reach the valley, and now, in the beginning of October, the early chill was apt to linger.

The sunlight was coming, though. He saw it in the west where it was backing slowly up the valley as the sun reached over the range in back of them. It filled the valley with a golden light, the hills, the spreading trees, the bottoms where the grass had died and whitened, and the small adobe houses with their scarlet strings of chili peppers.

It was a golden land, he thought, and then he did not want to think about it any more. To think of it with any pleasure now, to view it with enjoyment and to mark the beauty of it seemed a sin. That he had lived in it the time he had, had taken land in it and even built a house in it and leveled fields, while Stone still lived to do the things he did, seemed to border on some kind of crime.

He was ridden with a sense of failure and of guilt. The failure was related to the definite confirmation that the night at Anders' place had been for nothing, that all he had tried to accomplish there had been to no purpose.

It was all very well to say he had meant to put his yesterdays behind him—now, once more, the urge to finish Stone was strong within him. Pike had been the one to pay for his failing to act upon it before this.

They rode in a line, Alfredo and Alec abreast, with Maria trailing. Maria smoked and kept the silence of her thoughts, the dark rebozo hanging to her ankles, her strong face dark and stolid. Sometimes they talked, but not until their thoughts became so heavy that they must be shared.

"How will you know where to find Stone?" Alfredo said one time.

"I'll find him, all right," Alec said. "It won't make any difference where he is. The Guadalupes, or where—it won't matter any."

"The troopers have been looking for him, too," Alfredo said. "And have they found him?"

"It don't matter about the troopers, either," Alec said. "Maybe they don't know where to look, or how. Still, it makes no difference. I'll just keep on until I find him. Somewhere he'll show himself. Or maybe he'll come looking for me."

The matter was settled and he knew it. The time involved did not make any difference, no more than did the distance he might have to travel. He would spend the rest of his life looking for Stone if he had to.

"You make it sound like a long winter, friend," Alfredo said. "I like to spend my winters by the fire. How will we look in the mountains with icicles hanging from our ears, I ask you?"

"I told you once I was dropping you at Pike's place," Alec said.

"*Que va,* what will I do there?"

"I thought you were going to see to his wife, or don't you remember that?"

"Oh, yes, I remember—but I think differently now. Let Maria take care of the wife." He smiled. "I will take care of you."

"How do you know there is a wife?" Maria said behind them. It was the first she had spoken in an hour.

Alec said, "We all of us heard him say he was goin' to marry her."

Alfredo squinted at Maria. "What do you say to that, my little dove?"

"You heard him say that he planned to ask." Maria arranged her rebozo to a better line across her shoulders. "I would not marry him," she added.

"Have you had the opportunity to choose?" Alfredo said.

"No, but I would have no doubts."

"How come you wouldn't?" Alec said. "What's the matter with Pike?"

He was surprised, and mildly irritated, too—it was as if the guilt he felt meant he must now defend the memory of Pike against whoever might seem critical of him.

"He was too young and there were too many things in his head," Maria said. "He did not know his mind when we saw him. You heard him talk. I think this old man Jud, of whom he spoke, might have taken him along had he wished to. He was worse than *mia alma,* here."

"*Caray!*" Alfredo said. "How can you talk that way? Are we not together?"

"Now we are," Maria said. "But you were gone a long time. Altogether, you were gone some years."

"So, but the money was good to have," Alfredo said. "It bought a bull for us, a fine bull. And you have a rig to ride in, too."

"What a thing, indeed. I would rather have you at home, than any bull or rig."

Alfredo said, "There were my friends." He shrugged and put his hands out with the palms turned upward. "I ask you, could I leave my friends?"

"You left your wife, my little dove," Maria said. "And more, it pleased you—you enjoyed it." She put up her hand before Alfredo could interrupt. "Do not mistake me—I have no anger any more. But I would not put up with it again. I understand about you men."

Like a frog who puffs to bellow, Alfredo drew a deep breath, then let it slowly out. He took his eyes away from Maria and looked at the mountains, far off over the valley in the west.

"That was long ago," he said. "I was younger then. Now, it is all changed."

"I know," Maria said. "But now you know how I think of Pike. There were in him the same things that I saw in you."

Alec had never thought to wonder if the girl had married Pike—it was enough that Pike had spoken of it. And no matter he'd known the youth of Pike, his dilly-dallying with a thing, and the shadow of his yondering—it was like a woman to look at these things as doubtful omens.

It was enough to make him wonder if Pike and the girl had got married, after all—but then, no sooner had he wondered that than he could feel a rush of guilt. It was almost as if he wished she hadn't married Pike—as if a part of his mind had entertained some treachery.

They crossed the width of the plain that day, and in the evening they went into camp at a point above the river. In the morning they descended to the river and went on among the fields and trees that lay along the banks. Save for the brass and copper of the colors, the country lay much as he remembered it when he had gone north in early summer—sometimes they passed pueblos on the far banks where Indians danced their harvest-time fiestas; there were the little houses with their blue doors, drifts of sunlit leaves in dooryards, plumes of blue smoke winding in the branches, and cattle browsing on the old brown stubble in the fields.

These were quiet and peaceful scenes, and though he had no right to think of quiet and peace, or of contentment, still he thought of them, and of his valley where there had been such promise of those things. But then he knew that any kind of promise was only an illusion, something of his own mind, a wish.

The only real thing was Stone, and he was bound to Stone, and all that Stone had done. Any peace that came would have to wait, but now he was so full of Stone and what the man meant for him that he could hardly imagine a life without the latter in it somewhere. It seemed, now that he let his mind run off with it, that Stone reached into his past as far as he could see, and into his future, too. Stone and trouble, Stone and violence, Stone and evil—all the bad things that denied the good, fighting, killing, running. He was tired beyond all knowing just to think of it.

It never occurred to him that Stone was tired of it, too.

At noon they were going through a village, nestling sun-warmed and lazy in this lower country. Dogs snoozed at doorways and horses stood at tie-rails with their eyes closed and a foot cocked, only their tails moving. The angle of the sun made all the shadows draw up short, and any people who were out kept close against the low buildings.

They were almost through the village, riding in single file along the dusty road, when Alec saw the horses. They stood together at a tie-rail before a small cantina, half asleep, their heads bent down. One of them was strange to him, but he knew the runty hammerhead Stone had always ridden. The other would be Clint's and, being new, was likely stolen.

He put up his hand, so that they halted.

"Oh-ho," Alfredo said, pulling up abreast. "So they are here, in this place. How do you like that?"

"I like it," Alec said. "I like it fine. The sooner the better suits me—and this is a good enough place for it."

"A fine place," Alfredo said lightly, speaking in a tone he often used when action promised.

Alec was getting down now, lifting his leg across the cantle, putting his foot on the ground. He felt oddly happy and fulfilled, almost the feeling he had known when he had seen his mountain valley for the first time. Turning the sorrel about, he held the reins up to Alfredo.

"Take her and go," he said, smiling. "Go to Lorenzo. He knows his horses—you can count on her for anything. Take her now and go."

But Alfredo wouldn't take the reins, nor did he make any move to go away. He was dismounting himself.

"How you talk," he said. "What do you think they are doing here, *amigo*? Do they run? No. They are coming north. It is better that we fight together than fall alone."

"You're only guessing," Alec said. And then, as if time made argument a luxury, he turned to Maria. "Get him away from here, Maria. He's a fool to stay, and I don't want him here when they come out."

"Yes, he is a fool in many ways," Maria said. She looked around her at the dusty street and buildings, seeing them, yet seeming to see beyond them, too, in some way. "But perhaps he is not so foolish now. However it goes, it is well to end it now."

It was as though she had had it in her mind for quite a while. Alec was surprised at first to see such calmness in her—then he was not surprised. What had been a possibility had come to be inevitable and she accepted it.

"Ah, that is my love," Alfredo said. "You see, she knows it, too."

This was not what Alec wanted, but hardly had he thought to make a fight of it than time was altogether gone. Clint and Stone came out of the open door of the cantina and stood blinking in the sunlight. They were blind to the glare at first, and during the second it took for them to see again, Maria reached and gathered together the reins of Alec's and Alfredo's horses.

The movement of the animals as she led them off the road drew Stone's attention. Neither he nor Clint seemed surprised to see Alec and Alfredo; it was plain they understood. They moved slowly from the building toward the center of the road, with six or seven feet between them. When they halted, they were both directly in the sun, with Clint nearest to the barroom.

There was a moment when it seemed that time stopped, too. As they came to face each other across the dozen yards or so, Alec felt a leisure coming over him. It was as if time held itself apart from them so they might study one another before it caught them up again.

Neither one had changed much that he could see. Stone still had that sullen look, that look of a brooding bear. He still wore those same old shabby clothes—dark pants stuffed into battered boots, faded, shapeless shirt so steeped in sweat and weather you could hardly guess the color of it, soiled hat gone nearly black with grease and sweat around the lower crown. Stone's face could stand a shaving, too, the way it always could.

Clint, too, now Alec let his eyes pass over him, seemed pretty much as before. Clint had always had a hungry look to him, in the way of a coyote or a buzzard being hungry. Let Clint turn the sharpness of his face upon you and you had the feeling you were being judged for dinner—that he was sizing up your weight as eating flesh, or how the juice ran in your marrow bones.

Yet there was a difference in him, too, it seemed—his eyes showed a memory of Alec's thumbs against his throat, and of the ragged edge of death. A man remembered such things.

"Hello, Alec." It was Stone said it, the first that anyone had spoken. There was hardly a reason for words, but it was like Stone to want to talk a while.

"Hello, yourself," Alec said. "Fancy seeing you here."

"I could say the same," Stone said. "I had in mind to find you at Alfredo's place. We was headin' north, me an' Clint, comin' to call."

"Well, I guess I ought to thank you," Alec said. "No reason you should take the trouble, though. I was coming to look for you. I hardly thought you'd be so handy, though. I had a vision of riding the winter out. I was told you was on the fly."

"Was, but ain't no more. A man gets tired of runnin', Alec. That's how come I was on the scout for you. After you, I'm pullin' for Mexico. Let the troopers sniff the border, if they like."

It was a queer kind of conversation. They had come to kill each other, if they could, and were chatting like old ladies over a cup of tea.

Alec felt the sunlight on him in the dusty street. The heat of it bore upon his shoulders and his back, and sweat was oozing down his flanks. His ears picked up the little sounds around him; nearby, a horse put down its shod hoof upon a stone; farther off, beyond the buildings, a dog set up a barking; somewhere a turkey cackled in a pen, and to his mind there came the wild ones up among the oak trees in his valley. Just to think of it brought up the guilt in him again, but not so badly any more, for he had left it of his own will. Maybe it was never meant for him to have, but he had no regrets about it any more. It was enough that he should have the pleasure of its memory, the planning and the building of it. In the end, you always settled for less.

Beside him, he could hear Alfredo breathing.

While these things were moving through his mind, Alec kept his eyes on Stone and Clint. He watched to see which one would break.

Clint finally did. His eyes showed a sudden fear. Alec watched it growing in him, knowing that it soon must swell beyond the point where Clint could bear it any longer.

Suddenly Clint's mouth was closed to scarcely a rip, his teeth clamped tight against the building pressure; as it gave, a yell came out of him like steam exploding from a bursting boiler. Then he made a sidewise jump toward Stone, as if the fear in him would not allow him to stay put. As he moved, his hand forked down to grab his gun.

Everything changed when Clint let out the yell and jumped. The action speeded up, so that the eye could hardly follow all that happened—it could only take in parts of it. What he saw and heard and felt were all impressions that came so fast they had no proper order. Dust jumped high in the road while the roar of gunfire slammed against the buildings and rolled back from them. A soft concussion wave spread over him and color splashed a brilliant orange in the sunlight. Then he felt his own gun bucking in his hand, his finger on the trigger while the hammer rose and fell under his thumb.

He was hardly thinking of what he was doing. Though it was all over in seconds, he had the feeling of a long time passing by. Clint's jump had carried him into Stone, where Alfredo's bullets felled him, jerking. Stone staggered and the road heaved dirt in front of Alec as Stone fired. Stone then took his gun in both hands, but as he raised it Alec let his hammer fall, and then the fast-moving picture slowed again. Stone put his legs apart and his hands went loose about the butt of her revolver. His face took on a look of childish wonder, like he knew that something odd was going on and was puzzled by it. He began to walk away stiffly, then blindly, he stumbled over Clint and Alec's second bullet bore him down.

Alec stood in a silence bigger than all the silence of the mountains. Beyond him, Stone and Clint were sprawled in the dusty road, and in the silence of that moment he tried to find elation in himself—or some kind of satisfaction. But he couldn't. Stone and Clint were dead, and not a mark showed on himself or on Alfredo. They stood together, still, with their revolvers seeping smoke, just beginning to find the wonder of being alive. But he lacked even the gratitude for that. Neither was there any feeling of release.

What he felt was queer and strange, and only slowly did he work it out. Not until he went to Stone did he know what it was. Then he knew, and felt cheated. Stone was dead, all right, but save for avenging Pike nothing had been solved, nothing gained. The killing was too late to help himself. He was still one of the hunted. The curse of Stone went on and on.

CHAPTER TWENTY-ONE

THE NIGHT was dark, for there was only a sickle of new moon in the sky, and as he looked out through the window of the small adobe house where Jud had lived, Alec could make out the black shapes of the trees against the stars. The stars were near and brilliant, but their light lacked range, and the heads of the trees were only blots without shape.

Inside the room the light was better, but poor still. The oil lamp had been dimmed so that only the top of the wick showed up between the metal lips. There was a feeling of darkness, too, in the mood that rested on Alec, Maria and the girl.

The girl sat on a little bench against the wall, Maria in a chair beside the table where the lamp was standing, and Alec leaned against the window sill. The place was small and sparsely-furnished, but Ruth had kept it neat and clean despite the slovenly ways of Jud.

"You can turn the lamp lower if you like," Ruth said. "I expect they'll see it from the road."

"It don't make any difference," Alec said.

"They went by before," Ruth said. "They'll be coming back some time."

"Alfredo is out there," Maria said. "He will give us warning."

Alec said abruptly, "It was my fault, all of it."

"I don't know that you should take it on yourself," Ruth said quietly, sitting straight and still and gazing at the slender flame of the lamp.

"Yes, I should—it was me brought it on when I made a wrong guess on Stone. Or maybe I didn't guess at all. Once I went away from here, I didn't think about him much. Maybe I wanted to think him dead, and it was easier if I put him out of my mind."

He stopped and looked at her, but she was quiet. He might have put poorly what he was trying to say, but it was the way that things had happened, and it was truthful. He watched his hands, seeing their knuckles whiten.

"I should have searched him out," he said. "I'd have found him, all right. I knew all his hideouts, all the places he might go—his habits, too. I was told before I'd have to do for him, and I didn't. Not in time. But I should have, and then I should have faced the rest of it—like you told me once."

"I wouldn't say that again," Ruth said. "A person learns things, living a time in a place. Pike told me things about you, and others did, too, from time to time."

"All the same, it would have fixed it—for him at least."

She said, "A lot could have happened, though, to make things go wrong. You can't know about might-have-beens—but I know what happened here. It was my fault, too, you see." She raised her hands to her face, then took them away again and looked at him. "Did you know Pike asked me to marry him?"

Alec sat up straighter and put his hands on his knees. "He spoke of it—" he was aware of speaking carefully—"that time he came to visit."

"Well, he did. And I declined."

"Ah," Maria said from her chair.

But Ruth paid no attention to her.

"I declined. I hardly knew what to say. He'd been good to me while I was here and I liked him, but I didn't love him. I tried to tell him that, but you know how hard it is to tell a person that and still not hurt him. He was hurt, and badly. In the way a boy is hurt."

"A boy," Maria said and smiled. The remark startled Alec. Her previous estimate of Pike came into his mind. Now her smile seemed to convey satisfaction.

"Please—" Ruth put out her hand—"let me finish."

"Of course," Maria said. "Finish it, my little dove."

"He was hurt and went away. He was gone for two days and I didn't see him again until they brought him in. Word came of him, though—from every cantina to Bernalillo and beyond. Stone and Clint found him in one of them."

Maria went over and sat with her and put her arms about her.

"There, child," Maria said. "I understand it all. The fault is not yours. Everything will be all right."

"But, don't you see—if I'd felt differently, he wouldn't have gone away. Or even if I'd been able to tell him better. At least, he might have had his wits about him when he met Stone. As it was—"

Maria crooned, "Do not take it this way. It could not be helped. We understand these things, we women, even if men do not."

Alec sat in the corner on the narrow bench under the window, hardly knowing what he thought. He could not tell if he felt better, or worse, or what. Far back, Stone had said that Pike was overly fond of boozing, and it was probably the only true thing Stone had ever said.

Alec felt full of complicated emotions and thoughts, and some of them were not attractive. They gave rise to the feeling of guilt again, so that, when the sound came to his ears, he almost felt relieved to hear Alfredo pounding toward them from the main road.

Outside there was a flurry of hooves and harness. Then the door rammed wide, and Alfredo came into the room. He stopped, catching the door with his heel, and slamming it shut, cutting his eyes around for Alec.

"They come!" he said. "They are not a mile away. They are sure to turn in here. Now is the time to go!"

Alec stayed where he was.

"Go ahead if you like," he said. "I'm staying."

"*Hola!* Are you crazy, man? They will be here in a minute! Come on, while there is time. We can be over the river if you hurry!"

Alec said, "I ain't runnin' any more."

"But, why?" Ruth said. "What will you gain by staying? How will that fix anything?"

Alfredo said, "Crazy man, come on. The time is going."

Alec was able now to separate his thoughts and feelings. Perhaps he'd paid his debt to Pike, perhaps not—perhaps there had never been a debt. Maybe it was even meant for Pike to fall on bad times some other way.

"I'm tired of runnin'," he said, and remembered the way Stone had said it. It was as simple as that. "Being on the dodge is worse than death."

"*Amigo,*" Alfredo said. He crossed the room and spoke as though to a little child. "Alec, think of the mountains. Think of your fine place that you built, built with your own hands. Think of your fields and your house, and all of your plans." He shook his head. "What of them? How can you throw them away like this?"

Alec said, "When I left them to hunt for Stone, I was of a mind to give them up. I had it settled. It's better to keep it settled. It'd be no life to go back there again and always know that I was wanted and that they might find me."

He moved his hands, trying to find the words he wanted—words were always hard for him. "A man gets tired, is all. He can only run so long. Comes a time and there's nothing he can do but turn and face what is chasing him—no matter what it is."

"So!" Alfredo raised his hands and let them fall. "Of all the fools. Well—" He stopped as they began to hear the growing sound of horses. They were coming on the narrow track from the main road, coming at a trot, not in any hurry, but business-like all the same.

Alfredo said, "They are coming. They are coming for you, friend."

And then they were no longer coming—they were there. Alec saw them pass the window—they were troopers, sure enough, half a dozen on a rough count. They halted in the dooryard and one of them gave a shout.

Alec began to rise, but Ruth got up before he did and crossed the room.

"Let me talk to them," she said.

"What for?" Alec said. "I know what they want."

He began to follow her, but Maria stepped in front of him and when the door closed after Ruth, Maria leaned upon it, facing him.

"A lot you know," she said to him. "If you knew half of what you think you know, you would be wise. You men!"

"Come on, Maria," Alec said. "What's the good of all this?"

He made as though to pass her, but she spread herself across the door to block him.

"You will not get through this door, my friend," she hissed. "You men have had your fun. Now it is the women who will run things for a little while. You may ruin your life, if you wish, but you will spoil no plans of mine. I have had enough of that—now it is at an end."

"Listen—" Alec began again, and then stopped. An indifference came over him all at once. He was even too weary to argue with her. It was as if resistance of any kind had left him, and it was easy to think that it made no difference if he was out of the house or in it. When the time came, they could take him if they wanted him.

Now there was the sound of talk outside. Alec went to the window and looked out. A prickly-pear rose to block a view inside, but he could make the troopers out between the paddles.

There were six of them, still mounted. They sat in a crescent before the door, where Ruth was standing. He was able to see her, too, in profile, and remembered the way she had stood when Jonas had been killed.

"I don't know that I can help you," she was saying now. "I know of no fight here. I'm sorry, Captain."

The man who spoke for the troopers was a corporal, but the promotion pleased him. He smiled and pulled at his nose, and Alec could hear Maria laughing softly at his back.

The corporal-captain cleared his throat, putting his hand to his mouth, as if his elevation called for certain graces.

"Not here," he said. "I refer to one up the road a ways this noon. Some men were shot—a pair of murderers we've been looking for." He fingered his tunic, pulling the seams to an even line. "Good riddance, to be sure—still we have to ask along the road, here, for information."

"I wish I could help you, Captain," Ruth Hagan said. "But news is slow in coming here. I'm sorry."

"Of course," the corporal said, smiling while he bowed half out of his saddle. "Please forgive the intrusion. You understand I have my orders." He smiled very broadly as he sat erect again. "Were the choice mine, it would be different."

Somebody laughed and a lanky private leaned over toward the corporal.

"Hey, Captain, would it be your choice to ask about them horses? Beggin' her pardon, of course, but what would a fine young miss like her be doin' with three of them, all saddled?"

"I'm sure that's no concern of ours," the corporal said. "And, Ragen, if you don't mind, I'll be asking the questions."

"I'm not in the least offended, Captain," Ruth said. She smiled at him, and at the man named Ragen, too. "They belong to friends who came to spend the evening."

"Indeed," the corporal said. He smiled. "And please forgive the manners of these bast—of my men. They've been on patrol a long while." He put up his arm to alert his men for leaving. "I thank you very much—you have been most helpful." Then he smiled broadly with his yellow teeth, and winked at her. "We're leaving for Stanton, now we're finished here—a pity, if I might say so."

"Hey, Captain," and it was Ragen again. "Forgivin' my manners, sir, but why don't you ask her about the other one?"

"Other one?"

"Yair—that Winton fellow—that one at the fire. What about that one?"

"Oh, him." the corporal stroked his chin. "I doubt she'd know. You know what the feeling is now."

He glanced at Ruth again, and then, as though he thought he might as well, so long as he was there, he said, "This Winton—well, he's another we were looking for. There was a massacre—a fire—and he was thought to be involved. He disappeared, however, and now there seems to be some doubt that he was there. Or he could've burned in the ruins. There were some who were, and a few were never identified."

"Winton?" Ruth began. Alec could see her looking at the corporal and the men who sat about her, waiting. It seemed that she must think about the name and what it meant, of the man who bore it, too, and how her life had been mixed up with his. It was very quiet while she thought. The troopers sat on their horses patiently. Alec heard Alfredo and Maria breathing—he could hear himself, and he could hear his heart beat in his ears. Sweat broke over him, too, for if the corporal had it right it meant that he was free, and he was suddenly full of a love of life. Perhaps it had never died at all, but now that there was hope he felt it beating in him.

"Winton?" Ruth said clearly. "Why, no—I'm sorry, Captain. I don't believe that I could say about him, either."

There was sound, then—the corporal shouting to his men, the clatter and jingle of harness, of horses moving into a walk, the door beginning to open as Ruth returned to the room. Alec heard another sound, too—a roaring in his ears, as of the final breaking free of all that had been bound in him these past years—it all went out in a rush, in the way of a dam that gives before the load behind it.

He could hear Maria, though. Maria sounded very fierce when she turned upon him.

"There!" she said and glared at him. "She lied for you! What more can you ask of a woman, I would like to know?"

Now in the morning the trees along the river were full of golden light. The water was blue with the sky and with the slant of the early sun above the Sandias. The air was crisp with the hour and leaves came circling out of the trees upon its light motion.

The breakfast fire was dead. The horses had been saddled, and the one Ruth would ride had on its back a pannier with her few belongings. Save for her, they all were mounted now, waiting while she locked the door of the shack. When she had finished, Alec leaned across, took her arm to help her mount. She smiled at him, turning her head, so that he saw the quick shyness of it, and he felt a shyness in himself.

"Are we ready now?" Alfredo said. "All this waiting over doors." He shook his head at Alec while his mustachios rounded over his smile.

"I'm sorry to keep you waiting," Ruth said. "I don't like to leave it open, that's all."

"Do not listen to him, child," Maria said. "He is an old man who lacks imagination."

"It's only that I lived there for a time," Ruth said. "It wasn't much, but still I lived in it. Now I'm done with it forever."

"Of course. We women understand. But do not expect it of that old man. He has been three years in a thicket—though the thicket is now in the past. The door has just been locked on all that."

"I know," Alfredo said and looked at Alec. "Don't we?"

Alec bobbed his head, although he knew you could not lock the past away with any kind of door. But he had come to terms with his. It had quit riding him, at least; and time would help. And perhaps a day would come when all the rough points would be ground out of his memories and the regrets seek out their proper place among the other things that made the whole of it.

They were going up the thin trail leading to the main road. The world was good to look upon and he could feel the life surge in him as he had the night before. All the brassy, turning leaves, the stubble fields that had a look of being varnished in the streaming sunlight, gave out a promise of rebirth to follow upon the time of winter death. Almost he could see it in his high valley, the time of spring—the fields awakening to new grain, the creek in torrent with the melt, the little greening of the aspen leaves.

They came to the head of the trail, and where it joined the road they turned to the north. As they slowed, Ruth stood up in her stirrups and looked across her shoulder at the house below. She watched it for a long while before she sat her saddle again.

"I don't know," she said, as if a doubt had all at once laid a hand on her. "Perhaps I shouldn't leave. I don't want to be a burden. I've had enough of that."

Maria laughed, gently—in the way Alfredo sometimes laughed. "You will be no burden, child. You will be a pleasure."

Still, Ruth looked again, as if she must make sure before it was too late to change her mind. This time Alec caught her glance and, as before, she smiled at him, still shyly.

"Does he bother you?" Maria said.

"Alec?" Ruth said. "No." Suddenly she laughed—the first he'd ever heard her laugh. "No, he doesn't bother me."

"Do not think of him," Maria said. "He will not annoy you. He lives far away from where we do, high in the head of the valley."

"I heard him speak of his home," Ruth Hagan said. "The sound of it was nice."

"Home?" Maria laughed. "Dear child." She laughed again and turned to show her teeth at Alec. "Well, we shall see, perhaps. In a decent time, perhaps. It all depends. Winter is no good, but spring would not be bad. Perhaps we can go to visit him in the spring." She laughed again, and looked ahead along the road. "Spring is the planting season, child."

THE END